First published by J. Alanmars Publishing 2020

This novel is entirely a work of fiction. The names, characters, and incidents portrayed in it are the work of the author's imagination. Any resemblance to actual persons, living or dead, events or localities is entirely coincidental.

Joy Alantis asserts the moral right to be identified as the author of this work.

Designations used by companies to distinguish their products are often claimed as trademarks. All brand names and product names used in this book and on its cover are trade names, service marks, trademarks, and registered trademarks of their respective owners. The publishers and the book are not associated with any product or vendor mentioned in this book. None of the companies referenced within the book have endorsed the book.

First edition

ISBN: 978-1-64775-246-0 (hardcover)

ISBN: 978-1-64775-247-7 (paperback)

the goddess journal

dys
[FUN]
ction

A NOVEL BY
Joy Alantis

dedication

This work is dedicated to my daughter, Azareah York; a passionate, intelligent, beautiful, and amazingly talented soul. She is my greatest teacher who makes me laugh constantly. She has filled my life with purpose and many (mini) joys.

To my family and friends for always turning rough times into fun, loving, and memorable times.

To my love, thank you for sailing the ships with me in love and without judgment. Friendship. Companionship. Partnership. Relationship.

I am inspired.

Go within,
or be without.

Joy Alantis

contents

acknowledgement

Our Fathers Who Art in Heaven

To my Daddy, MacArthur. Thank you
for never needing a reason to love me.
b. 04.12.1943
d. 09.12.2018

To Yad. Thank you for sharing the best
part of you with me—our daughter.
b. 03.04.1970
d. 02.14.1998

Turning f[OR]ty

*"Owning our story
can be hard but not nearly
as difficult as spending
our lives running from it."*

- BRENE BROWN

Girls' Night In

"Did this muthafucka really just say that dumb shit to me?"

Finding a man who was down for the type of commitment Joye thought she wanted was becoming more and more of a chore. This was the topic of tonight's hen party better known as "Girls' Night In," when Joye invited her friends over for their monthly get-together.

Laughing hysterically, Joye blurted out, "I swear I wanted to punch him in his throat."

The room was pulsating to a playlist of the best of the 90s. It smelled like estrogen, Sangiovese, Joye's favorite, and pizza grease. The perfect environment for some kee-keeing.

Jordin, Kema, Mallia, and Ro could not stop laughing as Joye explained what happened with her 27-year-old chocolate boy toy she had been running about the globe with.

It's not surprising that Joye could pull a young man. She saw herself as a Goddess, and so did others.

Youthful and oblivious to her beauty, Joye had a petite hourglass figure, head full of thick, long natural hair, and piercing eyes, a man of any age would fawn over her. Joye continued with her story, "I wanted to say, 'First of all, you ugly!' but y'all know he's fine as hell!!" Joye and the ladies were literally falling over in laughter.

Joye's living room looked like something straight out of a magazine. Not over or understated but clean lines with a mixture of modern, glam, and rustic decor. Lots of white and neutral colors, a little distressed wood, gold trimmings, and bright colorful accents. The art on her wall ranged from pop art to spiritual art, including some professional shots of herself that were quite stunning. The fresh flowers gave it light and femininity that was welcoming. Everything was always in order and quickly gave the impression that someone very classy lived there. But not tonight.

The ladies turned that space into some silly and unrefined version of *The Oprah Winfrey Show*. No one was Lady O in this instance; they were all the hilarious and obscene versions of themselves going on and on about everything and absolutely nothing. No one cared if they gave good or bad advice. As a matter of fact, lousy advice was the preferred kind of advice during these types of gatherings. It just made for a good time.

Morals and principles were not relevant at this moment.

So when Jordin blurted out, "Girl you *should* have punched him, AND his ugly girl in the throat," then fell on the ground screaming as though they had kicked her, everyone agreed. Usually, Kema was the sensical and righteous one of the bunch, so she tried to bring the conversation back into reality. She reminded everyone that any expectation for this young man to behave any better than he had from their very first encounter, but she was immediately met with "Who asked you to make sense right now?" "You know you're always a buzz kill!" and "Can you let us have this moment please, Pastor K?"

Joye definitely wasn't trying to have any profound moments tonight. She stood up and addressed Kema directly. "It's fun to do stupid things, okay? I know this is ridiculous, but I just wanna do hoodrat stuff with my friends right now."

Kema yelled out to Joye, "Oh my God! You are so stupid."

Jordin and Ro shook their heads in disbelief but were clearly enjoying the entertainment.

Mallia was the only one who could remotely pull herself together to ask a clarifying question. "So, wait, can we get back to the Black Mamb—?"

Everyone shouted, "It's Black Panther, damn it!"

"Okayyyy! I'm sorry. I'm sorry! 'The Black Paaaanther.' So, this man, boy, child...whatever, chased you down and practically praised your name for an entire year only to finally tell you that you are too old, and he wanted better than you? Then you bump into him, and he is with a wack chick who is also ugly a-a-annnd could barely read?"

Blinking very slowly, Joye said, "Well, she wasn't *ugly*. I just didn't appreciate the way she looked. But yes. Yes. That is exactly what I am saying."

Jordin interrupted, "Wait. Wait. Wait! How do we know the girl couldn't read?"

"I told y'all when I walked up, she was asking the bartender for a pricelist! It's called a menu, bitch!"

At this point, the laughter had turned into high-pitched hoots and hollers. No one could believe what they were hearing. Joye was great at making her friends laugh or cry with her version of any story.

"So, she *could* read? She was just dumb. And you didn't appreciate the way she looked? Ma'am? Something is clearly wrong with you, my friend." Jordin said sarcastically.

Joye conceded, "I guess.

"But listen, y'all. When I sat down and pondered for two point five seconds about what had just happened, all I know is I turned into Denzel from *Training Day,* after everybody turned on Alonzo in the hood, and said, 'You think you can do this to me?'" She said, "Then, I was frustrated Denzel from Malcolm X," as she slammed her pen on the desk the same way he had in the movie.

"I was pissed off."

But Joye wasn't actually pissed off; she was just offended. She was offended that she had lost.

The ladies spent the rest of the night cackling about men, sharing their latest experiences, and making fun of each other's foolery.

Usually, when the ladies got together, male-bashing was off-limits. But, Joye didn't consider this bashing—at least not tonight—because, well, it was her truth, and she had to get it off her chest.

Ro reminded the group, "You know he's going to call to explain himself and apologize in like 11 days, right? I mean, he's always been unstable like that."

"I know. But I'm not going to answer." Joye grabbed her iPhone. "As a matter of fact, I'm going to block him right no—."

Ro snatched the phone from Joye's hand. "Oh, you's a damn lie. How you gon' block him, and he owes you some penis?! You've been over here waiting for him acting all virginal and shit. You better answer that phone when he calls. And...you better have sex with him one more time!" After speaking in an aggressive tone, Ro switched to her sweet girl's voice. "*Then* you can block his fine, stupid ass. Okay?" Ro handed Joye her phone.

"Yeah, like breakup sex?"

"Yep! Exactly...breakup sex." They all began giving each other high-fives as if they had just made a significant play.

At that moment, Joye realized that not one of her friends had any good sense...at all.

Joye walked into the kitchen to grab more wine. There was one bottle left: a red blend by 19 Crimes. Joye held the bottle up and called out to the ladies, "Ooh, how appropriate? Because I do want to murder that Negro." They continued to drink.

They continued to laugh.

They continued to talk shit.

As usual, "Girls' Night In" was a red-hot mess, but Joye needed it. They all needed that laugh.

ॐ

Jamel

Joye didn't think she'd be single again after turning forty. But there she was. Single. Again. And. Forty.

Three months after her 40th birthday, she met a very handsome young man on one of her business trips. A few years ago, Joye took a risky leap from corporate America, leaving a cushiony job as Director of Procurement to start her consulting firm helping businesses become more efficient and profitable. If a company needed to be connected to the right vendor, needed a new employee, or to train an old one, Joye was the person to call. She was an advisor and a strategist. She was organized and analytical and had a knack for identifying problems quickly. She was even better at offering solutions to her clients. Joye traveled and met people often, but she wasn't looking for a relationship. She was focused. She was trying to have a good time, mind her business, do an excellent job for her clients, and get back home unscathed.

She believed that all work and no play made her bank account beautiful, which is why she was a 6-figure thousandaire, but Joye always incorporated just a little playtime into her schedule if she could. She wasn't a huge fan of nightclubs mainly because guys tended to be all up in her face offering to buy drinks, and that environment just wasn't her cup of tea. Joye had heard so many horror stories of men's lofty expectations if they purchased bottles or entertained women at clubs and bars. She just wanted to steer clear of that sort of interaction altogether. But then there was Jamel. Surprisingly, she similarly met him in the same way she was leery of. He and his friends bought drinks and sent them over to her and her friend. She appreciated the gesture, but she wanted to get out of the situation quickly.

Her runaway tactics didn't work well because it wasn't long before he found her later that night at another venue in San Diego.

She relied on her attraction to him, and that was the beginning of their short but intense journey.

Jamel was only twenty-seven years old. That was incredibly young for Joye, but he was of legal age, and he was gorgeous, perhaps even one of the most beautiful men she had ever met. Jamel stood about 6 feet 6 and had smooth, dark chocolate-y skin. He had big brown eyes; the whites of his eyes made his eyeballs seem more massive and darker than they were. His teeth were perfect, and his smile was sweet. His barber must have been a close friend of God because his hair cut was immaculate. He had a thin manicured goatee, smelled divine, and dressed well. He could easily be a model. Jamel seemed too good to be true. But, of course, he was a good time, so Joye decided to enjoy him through her inner doubts.

With no strings attached, she paraded around the world with the young man. He was young, but he seemed to have his head on straight when it came to money and business. He co-owned a transportation company with his family. They worked solely with the Department of Defense and managed shipping for domestic and international assignments. Joye was relieved when she didn't have to foot every bill and act as his 'suga mama." So, from California to Panama to Dubai, wherever work took them, and everywhere in between, they would meet, and they would rendezvous...hard. It was a romantic and whimsical fantasy being played out: a perfect anecdote to a now middle-aged woman who could officially say she still had "it." For most, 'it' was all about the way you looked. By that definition, she wouldn't be wrong because, dammit, the girl still had it.

As with all relationships, there was a lesson she needed to experience to move into the next phase of her love life. She was enthralled by the idea that this man was utterly smitten by her, despite the age difference. It was the ultimate boost to her ego to be seen as sexy and beautiful by a younger man.

On the night they met, she felt strangely connected to him. In essence, his dark and deep eyes, his cologne--he wore 1 Million by Paco Rabanne, the way his hands felt when he touched her, the total energy of him was way too familiar. She questioned him—a lot—to see if he had some sort of relation to someone she had already known, which could mean she had met him before. That would explain the familiarity.

What is your family's name?

Where are you from?

Where is your family from?

Let me see your driver's license.

Is that your real name?

Have we met before?

Who sent you?

Joye was intrigued, yet she really didn't trust herself to behave with this man. She knew that if she spent any time, any time at all, with him that it would be trouble. Not trouble as in 'bad,' but trouble as in 'too much good.' Her gut knew this connection probably wouldn't lead much farther than a world of pleasure.

Or pain if they weren't careful.

Her heart fluttered, and her eyes smiled as she finished grilling Jamel. She had a quick moment of clarity and ran away to another venue, thinking, "God, no!

"Keep that man away from me."

The Black Panther

Joye was celebrating a successful project launch within her business, and one of her best friends, Kema, was able to join her on the trip. Kema was a Halloween baby and was kicking off her 38th birthday celebration while assisting Joye with work. Kema had a degree in accounting and worked as a manager for one of the local banks. She hated her job and said it was boring. Whenever Joye needed someone to check out the numbers on one of her projects she brought Kema along, that is, if Kema was available and accepted the rate Joye could afford to pay. They had literally been working like slaves in sunny San Diego from sunup to sundown for over a week. The client invited them to all of their events for the week just because. Meetings at fancy hotels, all-day conferences, champagne, and dinners on yachts, sounded like a hell of a good time and it was but they both deserved a night out away from work. Having a birthday among them was just the right excuse to forget about work.

Over dinner, Joye set the plan.

"We're making time to celebrate your birthday, Ke. Don't argue with me."

"I don't want you to feel obligated. Being in San Diego is enough. I've been having a good time."

"I don't feel obligated! Let's just go get drinks and look at people in their stupid costumes. This is our last night here. It can't be all work and no play."

"Cool. Let's do it."

"Now...I just need something to wear."

"I have a dress you can wear. Stop by my room and try it on." "A dress? Oh no. I haven't shaved, and I'm not going to. Unless I'm dressing up as the fuzzy legged lady. No dress."

"Oh, please. Who cares? These people won't be able to tell. I can't tell. Fuck them anyway. It's my birthday. We're just going to have drinks, right? It's okay to be trifling when you're out of town!"

The ladies got dressed and headed out, looking for a night of fun and laughter, dancing, and whatever shenanigans they could find. These cultured, worldly, Atlanta girls stood out in the crowd like a sore thumb. She was worried about her hairy legs and a second-hand dress from her friend, but the truth is, Joye could be wearing a hoodie with a baseball cap and leggings and still be considered beautiful. But tonight, she was stunning in Kema's one-shoulder, hot pink midi bandage dress.

Just like Joye, Kema was gorgeous. But unlike Joye, Kema had short hair styled into a pixie cut, and although she wasn't taller than Joye, she was just as curvaceous, and extremely confident, which added to her sex appeal. The Gaslamp Quarter wasn't ready for Joye and Kema. Or maybe Joye and Kema weren't prepared for The Gaslamp Quarter. Either way, the night was happening.

Joye wanted to make her friend feel special on her birthday and thank her for all the hard work she had contributed during the week. When they arrived at the first spot of the night, it was pretty dull. There were only a few people at the bar. The deejay was just getting started, so no one was on the dance floor. A small crowd had started to gather but there was nothing to see. The group of guys that were with Jamel were the only people who sparked a conversation with them, so they just went with it. After chatting and a couple of drinks they all exchanged numbers. The ladies decided it was time to head out. Joye was really only running away from this good-looking guy that she was afraid of, but Kema wanted to leave because she wasn't having a good time. So, when Jamel texted to ask where she and Joye had dipped off to, she gladly told him where they were.

Jamel: Hey. Wya? I texted Joye but she's not answering me.
Kema: We ended up at some club named Fluxx. You coming?
Jamel: OTW. You think Joye will be upset?
Kema: Nah. She's good. Come.
Jamel: Imma bring my boys for you!
Kema: Uh uh. I'm so good.
Jamel: lol

An hour later, as Joye was on the dance floor, attempting to mind her own business, smack dab in the middle of a busting a little move, someone approached her from behind and grabbed her waist. When she turned around, she was surprised.

"Why are you here?"

Jamel smiled and told her, "I'm here for you. I came here for you."

Joye was too tipsy from the Makers bourbon and ginger ale she had been sipping on the entire night to ask any coherent questions like how did he find her? Had he followed her? What did he really want? Or anything that would calm a person in their right mind about potentially being stalked! Instead, she kept on drinking and dancing. The only thing running through her mind at that moment about seeing Jamel was being embarrassed that he saw her a little drunk on the dance floor.

Once Joye accepted that Jamel was there, she began to appreciate that he absolutely came to the venue to see her. She embraced his presence. They danced. They drank. They talked. They kissed in the back of the nightclub. By the end of the night, she was holding on to his arm, tipping down E. Harbor Drive, headed to her hotel room.

Kema thought the entire thing was hilarious because she had never really seen Joye out of control. Since their college days at Georgia State, Joye had always been the designated friend who took caution to everything whenever they would go out over the years. She was the big sister in her family, so her parents always made her lookout for her younger sister. That big sister role spilled over throughout the years and pretty much into every friendship she had. She wanted to be the one who had it all together, but she was simply afraid to be the wild one in the crew. So, she took a front-row seat to it as if she was a den mother. But forty had done something different to her friend, and she liked it.

Jamel made sure Kema made it to her room. "Joye? You good?" Kema asked.

"Yes, babe." Joye hugged Kema, and as she walked away, waved and said, "Tomorrow." Meaning she'd see her tomorrow for their flight.

"I got her," Jamel promised to look after her.

Reluctantly, Kema smirked. "You better." She looked at

Joye and encouraged her, "Have a great time, babe. You deserve it." She licked her tongue out at Joye, smiled, and closed her room door.

Jamel and Joye walked down the hall to Joye's hotel room. Joye was digging in her clutch and dropped a few items on the hallway floor. Jamel bent over to grab each thing as it fell to the ground. He smiled because he was thinking, *She can't possibly be this drunk! Can she?* He stopped her and took her hand,

"Are you okay?"

Being a young Black man, he was very aware of his surroundings and the situations he placed himself in. Jamel wanted to spend the night with Joye, but he didn't want to set himself up for any problems in the future or rejection in the now.

"Yeah. I-I'm sorry." She handed him her room key and gestured for him to do the honors of opening the door. Even though her tipsy had worn off quite a bit, she didn't want him to think she was as uninhibited as she was about to be with him, as a way of life. So she pretended. She pretended and labeled it "fake tipsy" later on.

She intentionally took extra steps and slurred her words just enough to not resemble Thandie Newton in *Beloved*.

When Jamel opened her room door, she walked in, expecting him to follow her, but he didn't. He was smart about how he interacted with women from that perspective. He desperately wanted to come in, but he was careful, therefore patiently waited for an invitation.

All Joye could think about was every vampire movie she'd ever seen growing up. The ones where you are safe until you invite the dude with the white skin, black cape, and blood dripping from his oversized canine teeth into your life. Then you were bitten, and your life changed forever.

If there was ever a time when a woman silenced her logic, it was in a moment where a beautiful man was present. When Joye turned around and noticed Jamel wasn't right behind her, she took a deep sigh and gave in with her eyes. They shared an intense stare for just a few seconds. Then she stepped out of her heels and began to gently remove her dress. His eyes followed every single move she made around every single curve of her body as she removed each item of clothing. Finally, she signaled for him to come in.

As he walked toward her, he asked one last time, "Are you sure?" She answered with a kiss. She helped him take off his clothes and then led him to the shower. Even in a moment of passion, she was obsessive about cleanliness. She thought she could wash off any impending STD he may give her. From the shower to the bed. The couch to the balcony.

They were entranced by each other for the rest of the night.

They were loud.

So loud that the guests in the next room—or maybe it was upstairs—were banging on the wall to tell them to shut up.

They were wild.

They were rough.

They made "sex" because that definitely was not making love—until they both passed out.

Joye woke up, butt naked and wrapped in this familiar stranger's arms. The room was in disarray.

He had a soft snore, and his body kept her warm inside the cold room.

The sheets were thrown off the bed because they were

soaking wet.

Don't ask.

The couch pillows and their clothing were tossed around the room.

Her hair was a mess, and she was still fuzzy everywhere because Kema had encouraged her that it was okay to be trifling and not shave when on vacation. According to Kema's logic, shaving was for locals only. The best part was that Jamel didn't even care.

As soon as Joye shifted her body, Jamel woke up. He smiled and kissed her on her forehead. Then Jamel moved his hand across the side of her face. He kissed her on her cheek, then settled on her lips. "Good morning. Wow! You're beautiful."

She responded. "Hi."

That was it. Joye and Jamel took their time and made love like ordinary people instead of horny animals this go-'round.

They ordered room service.

Kema: Bitch! Did you die?
Joye: No, Bitch! I am a-fucking-live!!!
Kema: Ooh, I cannot wait to hear about this ratchet shit.
Joye: He's still here.
Kema: Ooooooooooook, hoe. We going to the airport or nah?
Joye: Shiiiiitt. Maybe.
Kema: Ha! Well, lemme know. I'll be downstairs at 1:59. See
   you then. Maybe.

They spent the next four hours sexing, eating, and in deep

conversation about everything, including the weird connection they both seemed to feel. Jamel didn't want to leave, but he had an international flight at 9 o'clock that morning.

He missed it.

Luckily, he was able to change his flight to a later departure time. Joye's flight wasn't until 3 o'clock, so they lounged around as long as they could before surrendering to the idea that they just had to let go.

Jamel scoured the room to retrieve his belongings. Poor guy.

His walk of shame began inside the room.

When he found his tee-shirt, it was stretched out of shape and had all sorts of makeup stains all over it. His pants were wrapped inside the sheets that were thrown on the floor. His shoes were under the couch. His underwear was in the shower...soaking wet. Neither of them had an explanation.

They just laughed and looked at each other.

"Oh, wow. I'm so sorry. But it's all your fault."

"Yeah, it is. Every time I wear this shirt, something crazy happens."

"Well, I need you to stop wearing that shirt then."

Jamel kept coming back for a kiss as he attempted to walk toward the door. "Unbelievable." He would speak underneath his breath each time.

When he finally made it outside of the hotel room, practically in the same spot he was waiting so patiently to be invited in from, he reminded Joye, "Don't forget me."

"Oh, I won't. How could I?"

As Jamel walked to the elevator, he was coming up on Kema's room. Kema stepped out, and they made eye contact.

Awkward.

Jamel smiled, nodded and said, "It was nice meeting you."

"Same!" Kema blurted out. Then she opened her room door and stepped back in. Chuckling, she waited until she thought he was long gone before she headed back out to grab a bite.

The girls met in the lobby at 1:59 p.m. as planned, and Joye decided to wait until they were in the Uber to lay out the details of her one night stand. *Last night was merely a night of lust and passion and would end up being just another crazy story to tell.* That is what Joye kept telling herself.

After Joye finished spilling all the freaky details of her lustful passionate night, Kema was shocked into silence. "I hope you're not pregnant with that baby's baby because I ain't heard shit about a condom!" Kema exclaimed.

"Oh God! Let's stop at a CVS. Do they have that here, sir?" Talking to the Uber driver.

"Girl, we got 48 hours. We'll get it when we get back home!"

"This is a sad shame. I'm too old for this shit."

"I'll tell you who's not too old for this shit. That little baby you were with last night!" They both laughed.

A few hours later, the texts began...

Jamel: Hi, Joye.

Joye: Hey handsome

Jamel: Did you forget about me yet?

Joye: Absolutely not

Jamel: Good. Because I can't stop thinking about you

Code-named "The Black Panther" because of his good looks, and his tall, muscular physique, Jamel appeared as a light that would dim rather quickly but not before she shared some incredible, mind-blowing times with him.

Over the next eight months, Joye and Jamel would create memories and contemplate the how-to's of their friendship. They would learn things about each other that they otherwise wouldn't share, and they would endure the fallout of poor communication due to the wide age gap and time zone woes. Joye lived in Atlanta and Jamel lived in Philly. They both traveled all the time, which was fun until they couldn't sync their project locations and dates. Eventually, they both came to realize that when the external pleasure of travel was removed, the relationship was for naught.

He wanted a surrogate mother, and she had fallen prey to the attention he was giving her.

After eight months of trips, their fling crashed in Philadelphia, where he showed Joye a bizarre and frightening version of himself. Jamel was in his hometown and things weren't as pretty as he had portrayed them. While there, Joye learned of a huge debt he owed to one of his business partners. He made it seem like it was nothing, but Joye would overhear him quietly discussing it when he'd receive a phone call. He was making money, but it was going towards debt and a lot of it. He was taking care of his entire family, so he was constantly having to interrupt plans to tend to his mother and grandmother, sisters, nieces, and nephews. Women were calling non-stop, and he drank all the time. He would get drunk and start arguments that just made no sense to Joye. Joye wasn't sure if this was just how the young folks behaved nowadays or if it was a clear sign that he was suffering from depression or some type of aggressive or abusive behavior. The way he argued frightened her.

Joye felt for him, but she also knew that he was just too much work. Young, emotionally wounded, and just beginning to try to figure out who he was, was a lot for her, not to mention, he wanted kids. And while Joye had said so many times that she'd give her husband children if he wanted them, she was sure that this guy, this young man, this walking battlefield, was not her husband.

≋

Monkey-Paw Prints

It would be ten months before Joye entered the "Forty and Fabulous" club, but it felt like it was approaching very quickly. Much like milestone birthdays are for most people, Joye was really excited about her big day. She was looking forward to the shift she had read and heard so much about when making a final exit from the dirty thirties. She had a few important things going on in her life. From successfully moving through entrepreneurship, experiencing the world through travel, and a game-changing six-figure opportunity in front of her that would double her income. A former client had reached out to Joye a few months ago and asked her if she would be interested in leading the next phase of their virtual reality project. The timeline for the project was one year. The client would be flexible with her schedule, but they required her to relocate to manage the team she'd be managing.

And then there was Abraham, the guy she had been casually dating for almost two years. He was named after his grandfather who died when he was born. He hated his "old-man" name, so everyone called him Abe. They had a few conversations about moving the relationship into the next phase.

"Hey babe, let's talk about this D.C. project. It's back on the table."

"Oh, it's back on the table, huh?" Abe confirmed.

"Yeah. And it's looking like it will happen in the next few months," Joye said. "So I just wanted to talk through everything with you. You got time?"

"Of course," Abe said. "You've made up your mind to do it, right? I think it's dope."

"Yes. It's dope, but how do *you* feel about it?

Abe didn't give her much pushback. "It doesn't bother me."

"Okay, but it impacts you. So I want to hear your thoughts."

"I said I think it's dope."

"Okay. I just want to make sure you understand this contract could literally dictate where I live for a few years. Are you going to be okay with that?"

"Listen. I trust your decision. It sounds like a great opportunity for you. If you're happy about it, I am happy about it."

"Okaayyy."

Joye had been giving Abe as many intimate details as she could about her potential move from Atlanta to Washington, D.C., for more than three months.

After being e-introduced to each other by extended family in a Facebook Group, Joye and Abe began developing a friendship online and then in-person about a year later. The two sealed the deal after several trips, long conversations, and a short-lived rekindling of a past relationship, all within two years of knowing each other. With her new beau in tow, there was no way she would make such a huge life decision without consulting with the man in her life.

Abe listened to Joye explain how she felt about the pending move. He had been working to build a stable relationship with her. Abe was concerned about what a significant change could do to them, but he didn't express his concerns. Instead, he let her talk.

Joye wanted his support. She needed him to buy-in to the idea. Because as much as she knew she could walk away to do what was right for her, she was excited about the pending partnership and making decisions together. She'd laid out the pros of what the move would do for her career and portfolio. She discussed the excitement around a new experience, and the opportunity to be part of something truly amazing. Up to this point, these things had only been presented as a dream or as an aspiration.

"What are we doing for your 40th?" - Everybody

Joye: I sent you an email with the full plan for the party. It has the venue, the caterer, the photog, D.J., cake design, centerpiece examples, EVAREEEETHANG. Check it out and let me know if I forgot anything, please.

Jordin: You are crazy! Have you done all of that already?

Joye: Uh, yes! You know I know what I want! #VirgoISH.

Jordin: You are a true Virgo and I love it!

Joye: Hey, so, you know I'm moving to D.C. in March. I won't be here to do any additional leg work, right? That's one of the reasons I'm laying everything out now. Do you think you'll be able to do everything in my absence?"

Jordin: Of course! How many people are you expecting?

Joye: I thought only 20 people were coming to this last birth-day, but you saw how 45 showed up. I didn't even have enough seats! Negroes. Anyway, I think 80 people will come to the 40th...Maybe.

Friends and family were always anticipating Joye's next party. They are still talking about the first adult birthday party she threw for herself almost fifteen years ago: a rooftop venue overlooking downtown Atlanta topped off with a full open bar, catered buffet, a live band, and a D.J. A lot of people wondered, if she had done all of that for her twenty-fifth birthday, what the hell was she going to do for her wedding or a milestone birthday? Joye had no idea. All she knew was that she had never had an adult birthday party, had barely had a childhood party, so this was her big chance to show out—for herself. At twenty-five, she figured 'if I don't do it for myself who's going to do it for me?' Sadly, at forty, this had continued to be her philosophy. So on August 30th, seven days after her thirty-ninth birthday, she went into full birthday planning mode.

Joye was on top of the world. She felt like she was getting closer to "it"; whatever "it" was.

Back in D.C., things didn't really kick off as planned on the personal side of her life. Work was work. She was busy kicking ass and paving the way for herself and her new team. But at home, things were what she'd categorize as "blah."

Abe had decided that he also wanted to move to D.C. He was clear that he wanted to marry Joye one day. Her move to D.C. made him nervous about the possibility of losing her, so as soon as she agreed that the move was okay, he quickly found a new job with Pepco as an Electric Systems Operations Engineer. This set things in motion in his attempt at taking their relationship to the next level. With his haste and mastery of piss poor planning, it became quite clear that he wasn't going to make the cut - mostly because Joye was a planner - or at least she thought she was. And while she believed they were communicating fairly well, reality proved that was a lie.

Joye spent two weeks sleeping on a friend's couch waiting for her guy to arrive so they could house hunt. Comfort was vital for her, so she was anxious to find their new home. When Abe came for the weekend, they had earmarked that time to find and secure a lease so that she could hurry up and get off of her friend's couch, and he could start his new life with as little stress as possible.

Yeah, right.

"I can't believe we are talking about making accommodations for a fuckin' dog right now while I'm sleeping on a couch!" Joye muttered.

"Hey, I'm not just going to abandon my dog!"

"How are you so worried about your dog, but not me? You don't have money for rent! How did you think this was going to work?"

"I just thought you'd handle everything, and I would pay you back."

"Without asking me? So I have to foot the bill for myself, you, and the dog?" And it was at that moment that Abe knew he had fucked up. Apparently, everyone except Abe knew that when relocating interstate, or anywhere for that matter, you should be prepared to pay something. Pay a deposit, pay for a hotel because you can't sleep on her friend's couch with her, maybe first and last month's rent, groceries, a chair. Something. Dammit, Abe!

These about-to-no-longer-be lovebirds had a very tough conversation that night. At the close of the weekend, they had toured apartments in Petworth, Foggy Bottom, Brookland, Trinidad, Navy Yard, Southwest Waterfront, and a bunch of other District neighborhoods. There was so much gentrification going on in the District that it was difficult for a visitor to tell what was a good or a bad neighborhood. They decided on a new development in Navy Yard. Joye wanted something nice but not too expensive because she was going to keep her place in Atlanta. Although Abe had secured a job, he wasn't ready for the move. He couldn't contribute financially, and since he should have known Joye well enough to know she was a planner, he should have told her of his plans in advance.

Joye was disappointed, and she expressed her disappointment with ease to him. Being a better communicator was something she had been working very hard on over the last few years. She had a history of low tolerance for anyone or anything that didn't adhere to the way she thought things should be done. So she was proud of the progress she had made because a year ago, he would have been cursed out and emasculated for being a dumb, little dick muthafucka. But, growth. Yet even in the short celebration of pride, she felt for herself at the moment; she was still overwhelmed and exhausted. She was stressed out. She felt alone and betrayed, and she was beginning to second guess the decision altogether. *This. Was. Not. How. This. Was. Supposed. To. Be*, is a common thought in the mind of a planner/control freak when anything goes off-script.

"I think you should stay in New York." Joye snapped. "Don't come here."

Abe was shocked and hurt. "Wow! No."

"Listen, this is not going to work."

"Why? Is it because I made one mistake?" Abe was trying to understand but also wanted to resolve the issue and resolve it quickly. "Let me fix it. I'll be there."

"You can't fix inconsideration. You had all this time to get your money together. You could have said something. We talk every single day, Abe."

"You're right. It was inconsiderate, and I was wrong. I can't even give you a good excuse. I've gotten behind on some things and tried to catch up and move on to be with you...I just dropped the ball. I'm gonna figure something out, though."

Except Abe would never be able to figure anything out with Joye. Once she felt she'd been disrespected, she muted you forever, and Joye felt disrespected by Abe.

This was their second issue with bad communication and misunderstanding. Yet, this was the first time Joye felt betrayed by him. Instead of taking heed to the obvious red flag, out of a warped sense of loyalty and her part "fixer" mentality, Joye decided to put herself on the back burner. She'd cover the deposit for the apartment. She'd neglect the fact that Abe was inconsiderate. She'd ignore everything because Joye wasn't one to give up on anything or anyone until she had worked through all options, even if that meant leaving her emotionally exhausted. The "fixer" was now in-session.

What's the saying? We make plans, and God laughs. Yeah, God was probably cracking the fuck up right now, but the Goddess, as Joye liked to refer to herself, was undoubtedly crying. Sitting in her bathroom on the toilet with the door locked, Joye cried her little heart out, wondering if she could *"just send him back."* Growing up with a younger sister and living in a campus dorm during her first year of college, Joye had experienced living with people before. But that adjustment, that shift, that so-called compromise of merging two lives into one space under the guise of a romantic relationship was not what she envisioned in her mind.

So, here's the story:

Abe lived in a tiny apartment in New York City. A true bachelor in every way imaginable. No frills. Literally. He was a simple man; A man that didn't need much to be his version of "comfortable". It literally took Joye all of four minutes to glance over his furniture and other belongings before she ordered him to "throw it all away." By her logic, there was no need for him to bring things of old, things of little value, things that basically did not match the decor *she* had planned out in her head, into their new home or their new life. She designed the perfect kickstarter for a life she was determined to have. Her plan was good enough as far as she was concerned. And while she discussed it with Abe, she really didn't care whether he agreed with her because he truly agreed or if he agreed with her just so she could have her way. When she strategically suggested they start from scratch and build and buy things together, she knew he wouldn't oppose much. In her mind, that's what new couples did; they started fresh. She didn't intend to be manipulative; she just wanted what she wanted and knew he wanted her. He agreed — out loud, but he clearly disagreed in his head based on what happened next.

The new apartment in D.C. was professionally cleaned from top to bottom. Joye was a bit of a neat freak, some called her OCD, obsessive-compulsive disorder, the clinical term, and loved the appearance of order and beautiful things. She was still renting an apartment in Atlanta. The only thing she moved to D.C. was two suitcases of clothing and essentials. With the project only being slated to end in one year, she had no intention of walking away from her place in Atlanta. They were supposed to buy the things they needed to be comfortable together in D.C. Sounded simple to her.

As time got closer to the move, Joye was excited, yet nervous. However, once she moved and Abe pulled up with his moving truck, her excitement turned to dread. While Joye had meticulously prepared their new home, Abe's moving truck and its contents looked like something out of the 70's sitcom, *Sanford and Son*. Joye could even hear the theme music in her head, and almost clutched her heart, and said, 'Elizabeth, I'm coming to join you'.

Why is this happening? Joye kept thinking to herself, *How do I tell him to go back home, get his job and apartment back. I don't want him here. I changed my mind.* Abe had "packed" for lack of a better term. Actually, he had literally thrown his belongings into the back of a U-Haul. He brought every single thing that he had agreed not to bring (out loud), items that Joye had deemed could and *should* be thrown away. To add insult to injury, much of the stuff was in garbage bags, and in no semblance of order that would appear to attempt to ease the distress that Joye was feeling when she laid her bucked, shocked, and condescending eyes on his things.

Joye was anxious, annoyed, and stressed out. The immaculate apartment was now a transfer station in her mind. Joye was also dramatic. She tried to go along to get along over the next few months, and there were moments when her calmness and acceptance worked like a charm. But Abe was a bit of a slow study when it came to understanding the "Joye" of cleanliness and order and she was becoming less and less patient with him. They were no longer communicating in a stimulating way. They weren't going on dates, and when they did, they were initiated by her. It didn't help that she was laser-focused on her work and working around the clock trying to balance old clients and the new gig. If he wasn't going to match her work ethic and drive, she wanted him to step up in other ways. When he did not, that gave her another point of contention in the relationship that justified her disappointment and eventual emotional detachment from him.

Abe was failing miserably. He was taking an "L" in the *Joye of Consideration*, the *Joye of Finance*, the *Joye of Cleaning*, and just about every other area. He seemed to be spiraling downward, but his understanding of the *Joye of Sex* was unrestricted. It is where he felt most comfortable and confident, and she felt relieved from the burdens of her day. After all this time, this became the one place they could connect.

After the intense discussions and disagreements about curtains, furniture, bills, his bullmastiff dog, Jinx, the sound of his chewing, and the dreadful greasy monkey-paw prints he would constantly leave on the stainless steel appliances, Joye was not interested in the exhaustive process that she was bound by in her past. She made a firm decision after looking at her calendar that she would not be tolerating what she considered an inadequacy in fundamental relationship behavior. She wanted to enter the second half of her life on her own terms but mostly feeling respected.

While her man was standing there crying and trying to understand what was happening with them, she was laying in bed laughing like Zack Galifianakis from *The Hangover* in her head.

Joye had spent so much time focusing on making money and working to perfection that she really thought she needed her relationship to not only support her neuroticism but mimic it also.

Joye wanted to understand, so she reached out to Abe's mom in search of insight into his behavior.

"His ex-wife really messed him up." Abe's mom was disappointed in her son. She wanted to encourage Joye to be patient with him and work with him through what she called a "bump in the road."

"I just wished he had talked to me."

Abe's mom never missed a beat about not holding her baby boy accountable, so she continued, "I don't know what's going on with him. But after he got with that girl, he was never the same. She really did a doozy on him."

Joye muted the notion that somehow Abe's behavior was due to being scorned. Joye decided he was just not ready for all the woman she was. Period.

This was the guy Joye had taken her time with. She had done everything differently than those before him. But she still questioned why she continued getting the same results.

Abe's behavior existed long before they chose to cohabitate. But it was now amplified in the close quarters of what was intended to be their home under the constant scrutiny of Joye. It was over. She didn't want him anymore. He was no longer worthy of accompanying her into her new life, better known as 40. She had no love for this man. She was not in love with him. She tried to love him. It just didn't work out.

They were over.

As Abe made his final trip back to New York, Joye got ready for a long weekend trip elsewhere.

She packed her bags and headed to Atlanta to celebrate. Joye felt good and believed she had been fair, so she wasn't sorry about the breakup. Joye had no stress or fear. It was time for a massive birthday party. That was truly the only thing on her mind.

The Party

No *ex*-boyfriends in sight. No *new* boyfriends in sight. Just a room filled with the people who wanted and needed to be there.

Joye has spent almost a year planning this birthday party. She booked a beautiful new art gallery in the Villages of Castleberry Hill. The room was a blank canvas for her to create whatever she'd like. Her party theme was *Becoming Joye by Design,* so she filled the room with forty black and white gallery wrapped canvas prints of herself. Each image represented a moment from each year of her life from birth to date. The room was a spectacular display of an all-white party with subtle accents of gold and pink. The room was filled with all white everything; from the tablecloths to the flowers to the chairs to the balloons to the three-tier cake. The caterer draped the food station in white linen, stainless steel chafing dishes, and serving trays. She served delicious heavy hors d'oeuvres that included treats like flatbreads and Cajun stuffed mushrooms,

chicken and waffle bites, mac and cheese hush puppies, chipo-
tle ranch burgers, shrimp and grits stackers, and more. Even
the bar was white with white LED backlighting that made it
stand out in the room. She had a full open bar serving top-shelf
alcohol. Of course, her birthday bar included specialty cock-
tails made for the night: a white chocolate martini, to match
the decor, and a honey bear, because it was made with bour-
bon--one of her favorite drinks in her taste profile and honey
because that was a favorite of hers as well.

The deejay adhered to the color scheme and wore a crisp
white blazer as he played all of Joye's favorite songs.

When she finally made her grand entrance into the room,
she was overwhelmed. Dressed to the nines in her black chiffon,
floral mini Emanuel Ungaro cocktail dress, and nude Christian
Louboutin stilettos, Joye intended for everyone to stop in their
tracks and take notice of her for she had arrived. But it was she
who had to stop and take everything in. The room was filled
wall-to-wall with her friends and family from all four corners
of the states. She invited everyone, so it wasn't a surprise, but
seeing that they all actually showed up just to celebrate her
really took her breath away. Her mother, her sister, her family,
her friends, cousins, and colleagues were in the building.

Once she soaked it all in, it was straight to the dance floor.
The photographers captured every moment of the night. As a
special treat to the men in the room who chose to spend their
evening with Joye, she did a very cool thing and ordered the
Floyd "Money" Mayweather versus Conor "The Notorious"
McGregor fight and broadcasted it via projector on the only
bare wall in the gallery. The staff began bringing out chairs
and serving the guests freshly popped popcorn so they could

enjoy the long-awaited fight. It was a surprise for all, and everyone in the room was impressed that Joye found a way to give just a little bit more to her guests.

The night ended. She was forty, she felt amazing, and she looked stunning. She was surrounded by people she loved and people who loved her. Joye was satisfied and knew that she had earned and deserved every ounce of love that was poured into her that night. There was still work to do, and she was up for the challenge and ready to face the world as a woman who was determined to figure out who she was, what she wanted, and where she wanted to be.

෫

turning f[OR]ty

Finding the [OR] in Forty

Oh. My. GOD! I can't believe I'm 40!

I feel amazing. My party was great, not exactly what I envisioned. The bad? My photographer's lighting broke, so my pictures were doomed. Ugh! Only 39 of my 40 pictures made it to the gallery wall. And the video dedication that I spent a ton on money to get edited never made it to the screen. A few hiccups here and there, but overall I had a wonderful time surrounded by so many people who literally traveled from the four corners of the earth to celebrate with me. That was over-whelming. I feel loved.

This has been such an interesting and maybe even an amazing journey so far. The main thing that stood out about arriving at this point in my life is that I absolutely, positively never imagined that I'd be single. Surely someone wanted to share their life with me by now. But nope. I have spent a large piece of my life just choosing the guy who only claimed he wanted "forever" with me.

I served as the girl before the girl who became the wife.

I remember relating to Beyonce's song "Ring the Alarm" but being too proud to ever express it because that's just not who I want people to think I am. I'm not that girl. Right? I'm the strong one. The one who everyone called to say they were doing okay but never asked me if I was. Over the years, my pain and outbursts were so private that I think I convinced myself that they didn't really exist. That was how I used to get through everything.

I've gotten so much better. So much better at so many things over the last few years. They say 40 is when you become a grown-ass woman. They say that you inherit a right to be unapologetic about everything. They say this is when you begin to understand that "no" is a complete sentence. They also say 40 is when you accept being empowered to stand in your truth, whatever your truth may be. You speak your mind no matter what and no one can push you around anymore. I think I agree, and I think I like it! For me, the most important lesson of experiencing all of these things was accepting that they didn't always have to reign true. Accepting that I had space and time to make a decision or not make a decision. That part of me being initiated into the 40/40 club is that I could and should choose and not fall into a pattern where I share the idea of every stereotype thrown my way because that's just the way it is when you turn 40.

Bullshit.

I could choose to be pissy about being included in the ugly statistics about being a Black woman, 40 and unmarried, or I could accept that this is my life as it is today, and own the path for my future. So what if I'm single and unmarried on my 40th birthday? I'm still unbe-lievably desirable.

None of this defines me.

I don't need to place a new chip on my shoulder giving me the right to be rude and inconsiderate under the guise of being unapologetic about who I am. I am pretty sure that I will likely have to apologize to someone for just that reason — who I am. Not because I am sorry for being me but maybe because I am considerate or empathetic to their understanding or misunderstanding of me and how who I am might affect them.

Basically, just because "they say" a thing is acceptable based on my age that doesn't mean I have to subscribe to those things and blindly act in accordance.

I have a choice.

I realized the "or" in turning "forty". Forty gave me my understanding of my explicit right to go against the grain when I need to, not just because I can.

My forty gave me the responsibility to handle my "grown woman" power with care as best I can. What I feel and what I believed yesterday may not be the path I choose to take today. Does that make me a hypocrite? Possibly. But could it also mean that through a new experience I've arrived at a new understanding, therefore, requiring a change of mind?

Absolutely, possible.

While I am not perfect, I'm also not a monster. And while I choose to stand in what I believe; I try to be flexible. It may take a little stretching me to the level of flexibility I need to be at times, but I'm willing.

So, with that I am grateful.

Thank you 40.

chapter two

All the Queen's
[ME]n

> *"In love, no one can
> harm anyone else; we are
> each responsible for our own
> feelings and cannot blame
> someone else for what we feel."*
>
> - PAULO COELHO

Whose Mans is This?

Joye kicked off her day with an hour session at Solutions Center for Intimate Partnerships (SCIP), an on-site therapy and life coaching center in Midtown Atlanta. SCIP was owned by a woman named Dr. Dalaina Ellis, a powerhouse relationship expert. Dr. Ellis and SCIP had quickly become a premier resource for counseling, and she had assembled a dynamic team of diverse clinicians to help lead the way.

Joye was a little hesitant but committed to the process. If she said she would do something, she did it. Albeit begrudgingly, she saw things through—even to her own detriment. Joye agreed that Dr. Ellis was amazing, but Joye still needed to feel her out. Her initial decision to utilize Dr. Ellis started with a high recommendation from her brother-in-law, Kyle. He was also a therapist, but he knew Joye would never agree to seek advice from him. Actually, Joye was more impressed with the plush facility than she was with the doctor.

"Hi, Dr. Ellis."

Dr. Ellis met Joye at her office door and motioned for her to sit down. "Hi, Ms. Allyn. How are you today?"

Joye was annoyed by the formalities, as she had already asked Dr. Ellis to use her first name. So, before she responded, she shook her head from side to side to emphasize her point.

"Please. Just call me Joye now. I am pretty good, thanks for asking."

"Of course." Dr. Ellis paused and allowed Joye to get settled in. "How are you and the journal making out?"

"Oh, it's good. I like it a lot."

"Are you using it?"

"Oh, yes. Absolutely. I enjoy writing."

"That's great. Now, this is your time, and I am not here to waste it. So, let's jump right in. What would you like to discuss today?"

Joye was checking Dr. Ellis out. Each time she had seen Dr. Ellis, her hair and nails, her designer shoes, her tailored suit was put together nicely. She was thinking there had to be something wrong with this woman. She was picture perfect.

Dr. Ellis leaned forward and asked, "Anything specific? Or shall we continue where we left off?"

"Umm, no. Nothing specific. Where did we leave off again?"

"Well, we talked in detail about your career and your family. Maybe today you can expound on all the queen's men?"

Joye had loosely mentioned the term "All the Queen's Men" to Dr. Ellis during multiple sessions. It was her way of glorifying the clutter she had been picking up along the way as she traveled through relationship debris. Referring to herself as a goddess or queen was aspirational. She accepted that her behavior and life didn't always live up to such high standards, but she claimed royalty anyway. Joye had subscribed to the idea of turning lemons into lemonade and seeing things through rose-colored glasses. It made her feel better. She was resolute in faking it 'til she made it, in this regard. Joye knew Dr. Ellis wasn't buying it, but it was Joye's version of the truth, and she was attempting to understand more about her behavior. So she let it rip.

"Well, I have dated a lot. So those are my 'men' and obviously I am the 'queen.'" Joye jokingly used air quotes when she said "men" and "queen".

"Are you dating now?"

"Eh. Not really."

"What does *not really* really mean?"

"Umm, it means I'm not in a relationship, but I have friends that I can call for special attention." Joye wanted to sound like a real grown-up who was in control, but she realized that she sounded more like an immature child playing house.

"Okay. What I heard was you have casual relationships that are in place to satisfy your sexual needs on an as-needed basis? Is that accurate?"

"Well, kinda. I mean, I can call anyone for sex. Men don't ever say no to sex, right?"

Dr. Ellis was stoic in her response, "I wouldn't be able to answer that."

"Well, those encounters are not relationships to me. They're just interactions." Joye knew she was playing a game of semantics, and Dr. Ellis wasn't buying any of it. "Maybe the answer is no?" Joye shrugged and made a face.

"It would be helpful for me to understand how you define relationships," Dr. Ellis said. She leaned back in her chair, adjusted her glasses, and then continued. "I do want you to be mindful that any interaction with anyone, or thing for that matter, is ultimately a type of relationship. So, if you have someone you only have sex with that could be categorized as a sexual relationship." She paused to give Joye a minute to think about what she had just said, and when she believed Joye was still with her, Dr. Ellis finished her thought. "If it's just grabbing coffee with a coworker, *that* may be considered a work relationship...an associate if you will. Your relationship with your parents would be parent-child, while other relatives would be familial relationships. Do you see where I'm going here?"

Game over.

Joye's cover was blown. It was time for Joye to act like an adult. "Yes. I do. So the answer is I am casually dating someone right now."

"Okay. So now that *that's* clear. Why don't you tell me about your relationships with these men? As much or as little as you'd like to share. You can read from the journal you received or just talk me through it if you'd like."

"Alright."

Joye got comfortable on Dr. Ellis' couch. And in each session over the next several weeks she focused on the men in her life. She needed to talk through her past so that's exactly what she did. She opened her journal.

"These are in no particular order, except..."

The First

"...Kendrick. Kendrick was my first kiss, my first everything. He kinda looked like Chadwick Boseman. You know, the actor?"

"I do." Dr. Ellis responded.

Joye got a little embarrassed and spoke. "I'm just gonna read what I wrote."

"That's perfectly fine, Joye. However you want to do it."

Joye began reading. "I started dating him when I was 17. He was a year older than me and he was the first person I met when I left Chicago and moved down South to attend Georgia State.

"Kendrick was a sophomore studying Education.

"He was standing outside of the Student Center with his friends. I was on a full scholarship, so I thought I was "all that" as we said back then. I tried my best to ignore him, but he saw right through my fake grit and was pleasant and friendly. And, *that* smile. He had the greatest smile ever.

"I will never forget the first words he said to me. He said, "Excuse me? You look like you could use a little help. May I help you?" I wanted to say 'no' but his Kool-Aid smile won me over. From that moment, we became inseparable.

"It wasn't long before our little walks and talks around campus turned into more. One night Kendrick walked me to my dorm. He was acting all weird and nervous. When I asked him what was going on with him, he boldly said, "I want to kiss you." I didn't hesitate. I said, "Okay."

"He went all-in too. Tongue and everything. I'm pretty sure I was a terrible kisser to him, but it was the best thing I had ever felt. We laughed immediately when it was over. I think I was embarrassed because I really didn't know what I was doing. That was the official seal on the deal of getting my first boyfriend.

"Kendrick adored me, and he was proud that I was his girl. But Kendrick grew bored with school and eventually dropped out. His parents allowed him to move into their in-law suite, and I would spend much of my time there with him. His parents were frustrated with him because they saw him "throwing his life away." I think they thought I was a bad influence in his life, and they soon became annoyed with my presence even though I was doing what I was supposed to be doing academically. His sister, Rayna, was my biggest fan though. She was his closest friend and the one who really understood that Kendrick just wanted to explore the world and enjoy life.

"Kendrick talked about his dreams of traveling all the time. But we were poor college kids relying on our parent's support. We were learning about the real world and trying to figure out who we wanted to be and how we would fit into it. We had no clue how to accomplish much of anything at this time. It was a hot mess but also a beautiful ride. That road got bumpy real fast when his parents said, "No more support!" They told Kendrick he could no longer stay in the in-law suite and he needed to get back into school or get out.

"I was able to go back to my dorm, but I was only able to sneak Kendrick into my room a few nights per week. He would crash at some of his friends' places when he could. After a while, he got sick and tired of living like that and decided he was going to start his life's dream. Kendrick took some of the money he had saved and booked a one-way flight to Frankfurt. I remember that conversation like it happened yesterday.

"He said, "Joye, you should come with me?"

"And I was just like, "I can't just get up and leave school! My parents would flip!" We went back and forth.

"Aww, come on! You don't think they have schools over there?"

"Yeah, boy, I *know* they have schools over there, but I can't do that. Why don't you just get a job here, or enroll back into school, and stay?"

"Joye, I wish I could but this ain't for me. My life is supposed to be bigger than just Atlanta. I've been here since I was born! And my parents have been trying to control every step I make. I'm ready to be free."

"I get it. But I can't go. Not now."

"Well, meet me there! You can come during spring break."

"Now *that* I can do!" And I was really looking forward to that trip.

"A few days later Kendrick moved to Germany. He became my first long-distance relationship. Despite not having his degree, he stumbled upon a teaching gig. We spoke every single day, sometimes three or four times a day! My parents would yell at me every now and then about how high my phone bill was. Kendrick was my first boyfriend. My first friend in Atlanta. My first kiss. He was truly my first everything, so I didn't care about that damn phone bill.

"Kendrick was only in Germany about three weeks before he was in a horrific bus crash on the Autobahn. Word of his accident spread through the campus pretty quickly. I remember calling his parents' house a million times that day hoping it was just a dumb rumor or that it wasn't *my* Kendrick, but they never answered my call.

"I tried to stay positive, but my mind kept focusing on the possibility of it being true. All I could think was *our time together was way too short.* From meeting him at the Student Center, seeing him off to Europe with dreams of meeting him there one day to receiving that God awful visit from his sister.

"I was sitting in the common area of my dorm reading a magazine when Rayna walked in. She quietly sat down next to me. She sat there with her head hanging, and then she just said one word: "Kendrick," and in that instant, I knew something was terribly wrong. I began to breathe heavily and grabbed her face lifting it up so I could see her eyes. They were filled with tears, and I just remember screaming, and screaming until my lungs no longer had air.

"Our dream ended up being a nightmare. There were 48 people on that bus. Eighteen people died. It took me a long time to come to grips that Kendrick was one of the 18. He was only 19-years old. I still don't understand how such a sweet, loving young man, filled with life could meet such a tragic death. I have asked myself, "*Why him?*" a million times. I will never have an answer. All I know is I would never see him again. He was gone. I could never get him back. I had to live with the memories. He left me with so many gifts and so much pain. This was my introduction to relationships.

"Loss."

Joye stared at the word loss on the page for a moment. She had written over it so many times that it was now bold and popping off the paper. She slowly raised her head and sighed. "So, yeah. That was my first boyfriend."

Dr. Ellis' voice was filled with compassion, "That's a great loss for you at such a young age. What do you think it taught you about relationships?"

Joye was emotional and said each word very slowly. "That life is short. That time is to be valued. But to never have any regrets. He taught me to go after everything I wanted in life because tomorrow is not promised." Joye grabbed a tissue from the table and wiped her eyes and nose. "He also taught me to hold on to people a little too tight."

Dr. Ellis took notes and nodded her head up and down to acknowledge Joye. She offered a comforting smile and said, "I think we should end this session here. That was really good work, Joye."

At Joye's next session she wasted no time and asked Dr. Ellis if it was okay to begin. When Dr. Ellis said, "Yes," Joye dug right into her journal and began reading her entry about 'The Filmmaker.'

The Filmmaker

"I loved Ferst with what I thought was unconditional love, and he seemed to love me without judgment. From day one, I told him everything about me—probably way too much. And I could literally just be myself with him. Our connection covered all the bases.

"Spiritually? Check.

"Our beliefs weren't exactly the same even though we both grew up in a Christian home. Neither of us believed whole-heartedly in the teachings of the church and would spend much of our teenage and early twenties exploring something more than what our parents had passed down. Ferst had great respect for the spirit world and a genuine intrigue of faith. We found a commonality there. He was on a quest for knowledge, and I wanted to know everything about everything because I'm just nosey like that. Ferst was one of the few people I could chat with about whether or not God actually existed and not have a full-blown argument. Ferst's essence made me feel at peace and comfortable in our relationship. We were true friends.

"He was smart, he loved books and documentaries just like I did, and he had a sense of humor that was Richard Pryor level funny.

"A lot of my friends said that Ferst "knew how to handle me" when they attempted to explain the effect he had on me whenever he was around. I definitely didn't feel that I was be-ing handled. We just had a real connection. I mean, even over the years when we weren't dating and we met again as friends, he provided an energy that allowed me to let go, be calm, relax and really reboot. Irrespective of our intimate relationship, he was like an outlet for me. When I needed a recharge, I usually hung out with him if I could.

"Intellectually? Check.

"We were two well-versed, well-studied, smart asses. Gift-ing books and sharing documentaries about science and histo-ry with each other was a normal practice of ours. Sharing deep thoughts, dreams, and insecurities was oftentimes our pillow talk. Reading to each other was our quality time. We were two big ol' nerds!

"Sexually? Check, check!

"We couldn't keep our hands off of each other. He was so damn fine. He had the biggest and brightest smile with the cutest dimples. He had big, dark brown doe eyes and a bushy almost unibrow that was only cute on him. And he had this tiny mole on his right cheek that I used to press on whenever I needed him to stop whatever he was doing and pay attention to me. I called him my poor woman's version of Rick Fox. That doesn't sound like a compliment but for my sarcastic sense of humor I was definitely giving him the thumbs up because I thought Rick Fox was fine too. Hell, Rick Fox is still fine. Anyway, I felt compatible with him in many ways. I loved it when we laughed together and clowned each other. I loved watching movies with him. I loved listening to music and debating each other when our taste in song or artist differed. I even loved sitting and being silent with him. I just liked having him around.

"When life, loss, and distance began to show its ugly face the downside of us happened really quickly. Every time something bad happened between us or to us it was like he drifted further and further away from me. With each major decision made we jeopardized us. Eventually, I realized that we were compatible everywhere except when he started lying to me about other women. That was tough. Loving him was easy. Being able to trust him with my heart was so simple until he made it very, very difficult. I wanted to. I feel like I really tried. In the end, the infidelity was too much to bear. He destroyed the broken heart I was already carrying around."

When Joye finished that last sentence there was silence for a few seconds. Dr. Ellis was jotting down a few things in her notebook. She looked at Joye and then sat her pen in the spine of her notebook. "Did you ever forgive him for breaking your heart?" Dr. Ellis asked.

Joye took a deep breath. "I think so. I mean, I don't hate him."

"Okay, but did you forgive him for breaking your heart?"

"Yeah, I think I did. But there was so much going on in that relationship, Dr. Ellis. I just learned to love him in a different way from afar."

"Did you do that to protect yourself?" Dr. Ellis probed.

"I dunno. Maybe I did. I just knew I couldn't keep going through hurt with a man I loved so much. But I don't really want to talk about him."

"Okay. Okay. I respect that. When you're ready maybe we can go a little deeper about you, the hurt, and Ferst." Joye raised her eyebrows as if to say, 'No the hell we won't'!

"We still have quite a bit of time in this session. Do you want to continue reading your entries or would you like to talk about something else?"

"Nope. I'll keep reading." Joye grabbed a bottle of water Dr. Ellis had on her side table for her patients. She took a couple of long drinks of water, slowly twisted the cap back onto the bottle before setting it back on the table, and then began reading again.

The Nobody

"Soooo, next up, 'The Nobody.'"

"The Nobody?" Dr. Ellis asked.

"Yeah," Joye replied, "He was so wack I couldn't even come up with a name for him," Joye began reading. "I met him at the bus stop." Joye stopped and looked right at Dr. Ellis. "DO. NOT. JUDGE. ME."

Dr. Ellis smiled. "This is a judgment-free zone."

"Okay, good." Joye continued. "You know what, go ahead and judge me because I would definitely be judging you. TN-that means 'The Nobody,' helped me with the necessities of life, you know rides to the grocery store to get tissues and milk, and that which was cool." She paused and thought to herself *Good God, I was so young and dumb* before she continued reading. "But he moaned like a girl during sex." Then Joye started doing high pitched moans and groans to illustrate.

"He had a big dick, though." Joye stopped herself abruptly to confirm if it was okay to be so vulgar. "Oh, God! I'm sorry! Is that okay?"

Dr. Ellis let out a quiet laugh and assured Joye that it was okay. "Yes. You can be yourself here. Continue. Please"

"Good. Okay so, yeah, his dick was huge, but the moaning was disgusting. I have no idea why I even allowed that man into my space," she said, rolling her eyes. "Anyway, next!"

The Frat

"This guy wasn't about anything at all. He was just something to do. He was tall, dark, and fly--just like I like 'em. He was fun to be around. He liked going out and he knew a lot of people. It didn't matter if we went dancing or to watch a game with friends or had a cookout at the house, we were always going to have a good time. We both knew that our connection was nothing more than sexual chemistry. After a few months of casually dating him, which means having a whole lot of sex, I broke it off. We agreed in the very beginning that we'd tell each other if our feelings started to get involved. I knew that if we kept sleeping together I would eventually want more than sex from him. There was no reason to try to force a relationship out of what we had so I requested "breakup sex." He declined but called me back five minutes later to say he changed his mind. I met him at his house an hour later and he obliged me. No conversation about it. No strings attached. He had no reason to care that I was cutting him off because he literally had 50-11 bitches. He wasn't losing anything that he didn't have an excess of. I was just a piece of ass to him and I wasn't even mad about it because he was the exact same thing to me until I realized that even casual dating was a freakin' chore."

Joye seemed to ramble through the next journal entries as Dr. Ellis listened. It was easy to determine through Joye's tone that the next couple of guys she mentioned weren't very important to her, yet she found it necessary to include them in her journal.

The Boring Barber

Joye sighed, "He was a good guy, but boring. It was almost like I had to take all of the steps with this guy. When I fantasized about a future with him I knew that I would have to make every decision in the house and as controlling as I could be at times, that was a real turn-off. I remember one night when he took me out for dinner and how we sat across from each other at the dinner table in silence. My mind was racing with thoughts of all the ways I could easily cheat on him. I'm not even a cheater but I was so bored that I figured I would have to. I gave him a few opportunities to step up and show me that he was truly interested in me over the years, but he always, always let me down with his lack of initiative. Of course, he was a beautiful man. That's pretty much all I dated. He was tall, handsome, and he had this sexy ass New York accent. He was from Queens. Of course, I made jokes. I would say "Queens? Like Nasir Jones' Queens? Nah, son. You are from Queens, Wisconsin, nigga." No disrespect to Wisconsin, but...really? He was a perfect example of looking good on paper. He was from a great family. He was an educated man. He owned real estate and a few barbershops. He had a hefty savings, an actual retirement plan, was well versed and engaged in the stock market. He didn't have children. He was a responsible citizen and from what I gathered over the years he was a faithful man. But I could not get past the fact that he was fucking boring. I would, however, revisit the idea of being in a relationship with him often because I wanted to figure out if I could somehow fix or overcome the boredom. That was a waste of time."

Joye closed her journal and stood up. She stretched her arms toward the ceiling. Dr. Ellis noticed Joye taking a break but finished writing down her thoughts. When she lifted her head, she noticed Joye had taken a few steps and was staring at the paintings on her office wall. They were a series of colorful abstract paintings of a black woman. Joye turned to look at Dr. Ellis before she said, "These are really nice. Is this your work?" Dr. Ellis had six images on her office wall from this collection: *Who, What, Where, When, Why, and How.* Each picture was a bold depiction of a black woman's lips and nose but where the eyes and top of the head would normally be the artist had filled with abstract and vibrant splatters of color.

"Oh no. Not at all. I am far from an artist. Those are pieces by an African American woman out of New York. She calls this collection *Headset*. She has some powerful, powerful artwork that focuses on the emotions of black women.

"Are you a collector?" Dr. Ellis asked.

"No. I just love all things beautiful." Joye pointed at the painting named *Who* and said, "This one is, whew!" and let out a big sigh. Dr. Ellis made a note that Joye had a response to the particular piece of art.

Joye realized she had been distracted and quickly walked back to her seat. She picked up her journal and stated, "I want to keep going."

The Married Man

"I don't know why the idea of dating a married man was acceptable to me at this time but, it was. At least, for a short period of time, I suppose. He was intelligent and handsome. He also had a New York accent. Clearly, I like those. He took me on road trips up and down the East Coast. The best part was the money he'd give me to go on shopping sprees in every city we traveled to. I remember meeting him at a hotel one night. When he was done fucking me, he told me to "shush" so he could take a call from his wife. I wish I could say I was surprised that he had a wife, but that would be a whole lie. I knew he was married. I didn't begin to care until my feelings got hurt. After he hung up the phone there was no cuddling. No watching TV. He simply cleaned off his balls in the bathroom sink and went home to his wife. He told me that check out was "tomorrow at 11 o'clock", that I could stay until then if I wanted to, and of course, order whatever I wanted from room service. It was business as usual for him. Like taking out the garbage. The dummy in me got excited about the free room and the open invitation for room service and thought maybe I'd invite my girls over and have a fun night in. The woman that my parents raised felt cheap. What was I doing? I got the hell outta there and never saw him again. I was losing at life with this horrible, horrible decision."

The Personal Trainer

"He was my half-German, half-Armenian white boy toy. I think I was just curious. There was absolutely no love connection. No intellectual connection. Nothing. He was just a cute ass white boy who was in my line of sight. I was living overseas and honestly; I was just killing time. He was interested and I was like "why not?" I know that's a terrible thing to say but it was true. He was really cute and being a personal trainer his body was very nice to touch and to look at. He was like one of those Greek sculptures but with a better-sized penis. With the language barrier, I didn't have to say much. He didn't understand much when I spoke anyway and I couldn't care less about anything he thought or said, so it was a win-win. 'Do you have condoms?' was the only thing on my mind. I had sex with him twice and it was mediocre at best. The second time was just to be sure that I wasn't trippin' and that it was as bad as it was the first time. I wasn't trippin'. He really was a waste of sex. Maybe this was the sex god's way of punishing me for tapping into my carnal instincts under the false pretense of being an in control grown-ass woman."

Reading her journal out loud seemed weird to Joye, at first, but she was really getting into it. "How am I on time, Dr. Ellis?" Joye felt like she was just going on and on and was concerned about running out of time.

Dr. Ellis looked at her watch then directly at Joye. "You are doing really well. If you want to keep going, keep going." Dr. Ellis discovered early in their sessions that Joye really needed to feel heard, so she reassured Joye that it was okay to continue. "This is all part of your healing process. I don't have another patient for a few hours so take whatever time you need."

Joye smiled and continued to read.

The Other Frat

"There was something about those frat boys. Maybe it was the way they hop? You know? How they step and chant. Yeah, no. I casually dated Bryce after meeting him out at a bar. I was having an amazing Happy Hour with my white friends. If you have ever hung out with white people at a bar on a Friday then you know I was 'drinkin' drinkin'! Drinking and taking shots and more drinking... It was not one of my best moments. Just imagine one black girl in the entire bar acting a damn fool. As I rose up from laying across a table while some white boy took belly shots off of me, the Lord's light shined down on this one man sitting at a table filled with a group of other beautiful Black men. I sobered up so damn quick, dropped my head, and headed straight for the bathroom to clean my life up. His boy approached me and asked if I was okay. He said, "I hope you're not about to leave because my friend really wants to talk to you. He just went to the men's room, but he asked me to make sure you didn't leave." I was like 'cool', but I was really thinking *I hope it's the one that the light from the heavens was beaming down on!* Long story short: it was. Look at God!

"When Bryce came out of the bathroom, he introduced himself and we chilled at the bar for a moment getting to know the basics about each other. We exchanged numbers; he made sure I was sober enough to drive before walking me to my car. It was only a few weeks before we were hanging out regularly. And even though he wasn't exclusive with me, he did a great job making me feel like the only girl in the room whether we were at a barbecue, a sports bar, or a restaurant. He also did a really good job of making me feel like the most beautiful girl in the room. He complimented me a lot and about things that most men didn't even notice like my flawless, perfectly naturally arched eyebrows. That was nice. It made me feel like he paid attention to my details.

"I used to think he was sneaking upstairs to call his "real woman", but it turns out that he was really sneaking upstairs because he had diabetes and needed to take his insulin shots. Bryce didn't have to hide his diabetes from me though. I would have been perfectly fine with it until I realized he barely took care of himself. His eating, drinking, and exercise habits were not supportive of his illness. I was concerned, but ...but his ignent ass-yes ignent-would say, "We all gotta die from something." And I would always respond, "True, but why are you gonna let diabetes kill you, dummy?" Look, he didn't care about his health, and I was too fly to be pushing him around in a wheelchair because he had to get his feet chopped off.

"I really liked Bryce, but he was always honest about his lifestyle and wasn't ready to cut off his other girls to entertain a real relationship with me. He said he wanted to be faithful in whatever committed relationship he went into, especially his marriage, so we kept it casual. I was turned on by his honesty. I mean, he was already fine as hell, but he started looking even better after being bold and straight up about what he wanted. We messed around quite a lot over the years. He was definitely 'break in case of emergency' or what I call 'familiar dick.' He knew it and was fine with it. So that's what we did. Til this day, he still calls and texts asking to hook up. It's just a matter of time before I answer and fall back into this pattern."

Joye stopped reading and began flipping through pages of her journal. Dr. Ellis interrupted, "This pattern? Why do you think you will fall back into it, do you know?"

"No, not really," Joye was being illusive. "I only have a few more to go. I think I can knock them out in our next session if that's okay."

"Absolutely." Joye stood up and thanked Dr. Ellis and headed out.

"Same place, same time, tomorrow?"

Joye responded proudly, "Yes. Same place, same time. See you tomorrow, Doctor."

୫

Tomorrow couldn't come fast enough. Joye was focused on her therapy. She wondered what the outcome of sharing her relationship drama with Dr. Ellis would be and she was looking forward to it.

As usual, Dr. Ellis was in place and awaiting Joye's arrival. The office and everything in it was in perfect order. Joye took her seat.

"Are we jumping right into your journal today? Dr. Ellis asked.

Joye opened her journal and replied, "Yes, ma'am."

The Million Dollar Slave

"We only dated for a few months. It was exciting and fun. He made sure I had a floor seat to watch his basketball games whenever I wanted to attend in any city. I made it into a few blogs a couple of times because people were trying to figure out if he was finally getting serious with someone. Women, including me, were mesmerized by him. He was 6 foot 9. He had 3 percent body fat and his skin was like smooth well-moisturized, dark chocolate. His arms were arguably better than Michael Jordan's 1990s arms. He looked like a beautiful black god from a movie like *Shaka Zulu* or like what I imagined the African Orisha Shango would look like.

"The first time we "did it" he literally just took all of his clothes off in the middle of a conversation. I was mid-sentence and when I glanced up, boom, he was butt booty naked. My mouth was on the fucking floor. I was just amazed at how he looked. Good lord. So I took my clothes off too. He picked me up like a caveman and carried me upstairs to his bedroom. Anyway, he liked spending time with me because I was fine too, and I never made a big deal about his brand new $32 million dollar contract. That's because I really didn't give a shit. I was going to call him before I ever knew he was going to be rich. I met him at a party at a club in Atlanta. Apparently, he and his teammate were throwing the party. I was just there to dance. I was with my sister and after she saw me talking to him her silly ass was like "Oh my god! That's the guy whose party we're at!" I was oblivious. We laughed about how I had no idea and was just giving my number to what I thought was "any ol' body". Then she started quoting *Coming to America*: "The boy's got his own money!" When we finally stopped laughing, she said, "She always gets the good ones" and just like that we were laughing again.

"Our last time together was at a nightclub because that's what a lot of young athletes like to do--party. As the night was coming to a close, he asked me to meet him back at his house. He handed me the key, and I happily drove to his place. Something about having the key or the code to the house always made women feel like they were something special. I went straight upstairs and showered and prepared myself for what I thought was about to be some good sex, morning cuddling after making egg whites, turkey bacon, and avocado for breakfast in a few hours. But nope! I guess he got too drunk to remember that he had sent me to his house to wait for him because he never showed up. Yep, he left me there alone all night. He didn't answer his phone when I called to see what was going on and if he was on the way. My voicemails were nice and simple, "Where are you? Are you okay?" I started to worry because I knew he was drinking a lot. But then I began thinking, *This Negro is just a whore. He dipped off with some other girl.* After waiting four hours, I finally decided to put my cute little pink dress back on and leave. I also decided to never call him again. I left my key on the little table he had in his foyer and got out of there but not before thinking if there was something I could steal from his black ass. But I didn't take anything except the little bit of dignity I had left. He obviously didn't care because he never called me back either. I don't blame him. I mean, I'm amazing, but if I were a young, handsome, and wealthy man with plenty of women I would probably--nah, he was a piece of shit for that. He's still out here slinging penis."

The Mogul

"I think I was just touching all the bases with this guy. I had dated just about every type of man but an older one. He wasn't a senior citizen, but he was almost 20 years older than me. He had been divorced three times already so clearly, he was the problem. He would wine and dine me and take me to galas. He bragged about how beautiful, talented, smart, and reliable I was. Being fresh out of a marriage, he liked his freedom so any inkling of me seeming to demand accountability was shunned. While I thought things were going well and maybe even ex-pecting a ring because he was old and seemed like the marry-ing type, things took a turn.

"A left turn.

"He went on a trip to Seattle and decided he wasn't going to call me or respond to my calls for over a week. When I finally spoke to him about his behavior, he started yelling at me like I was a child. I was like, "I know you're old enough to be my father, but watch it!" Maybe he was mad because I told him that one of my reasons for being concerned was that he was old, and I was starting to worry if he had died of a heart attack or because he was just an asshole. I never figured that out. I ended that conversation with "Okay, I'm tired of you yelling. We're done." I hadn't done anything wrong and I believed at that time that yelling at someone was disrespectful.

"Go figure."

Each session, Dr. Ellis took notes with raised eyebrows, as she patiently listened to Joye detail her relationships. She watched Joye be squeamish around certain details and burst into laughter or get a little teary-eyed at times as she spoke about her "interactions."

"Is that all?" Dr. Ellis asked.

"Yes. I mean, there were a few ancillary and insignificant situations thrown in over time, but yeah. That's it."

"Okay. So those you mentioned *are* significant to you?"

"Yeah, they all had an impact on me. Of course, 'Monkey-Paw Prints' and 'The Black Panther' were rather significant parts of my life for different reasons because those relationships led into and surrounded my big birthday. But I shared that information already—. The others were not a big deal, but they did have some sort of influence on my life just in different ways, I guess. I can talk about them later, right?"

Dr. Ellis wanted to keep Joye encouraged and comfortable through her process of sharing. "That's fair. We will have time to get to the less significant relationships or anything you may have left out when you are ready. You shared a lot of information in your recollection of how your relationships began and ended."

"Really? I thought they were just highlights." Joye could make light of things easily, especially when she wasn't ready to confront the real issue.

"No. They were much more than highlights in my opinion. There were a variety of emotions, a lot of love but also disappointment. Your stories were very insightful. Thank you for sharing."

Joye asked, "So what do you think? I know how to pick'em, right?"

"I wouldn't say that. Remember, this is a no-judgment zone. I really believe your breakthroughs will come when we tackle what *you* really think about all that you have shared over time. I'd like to challenge you to not focus on so much of the details of the relationships or your choices in men. I want you to focus on you, not who you picked, but more so on how and why you chose these particular people as partners."

"Okay. I can try that."

"Let's do this. We are at the end of our time together, but I would love for you to continue this session a little bit on your own. Then we can review when we reconvene. Does that sound like something you are interested in?"

"You mean like homework?"

"Yes. Homework. Or we can call it an exercise. Whatever you choose to identify it as, based on what you just shared, I believe it will be rather simple for you." Dr. Ellis had to do a lot of negotiating with Joye during her sessions. Joye wanted to understand everything the doctor wanted, but she also wanted to protect what she wasn't comfortable sharing.

"Sure. What do I need to do?"

"I would like you to continue writing in your journal. This time take a deeper dive into each overview of every relationship we spoke about today. I want you to do only three things for each, Dr. Ellis said, as she handed Joye a piece of paper and an ink pen. "Write this down," she instructed. "First, list the top three emotions you felt. Next, list all of the common behaviors in yourself and in your partners during each relationship. And, finally, list at least one thing you could have done differently to change the outcome of the relationship. Does that sound doable?"

"Wow. Things I could have done differently?"

"Yes. Can you do that?"

"I will certainly try."

"Then we have a deal." Dr. Ellis lent a handshake to Joye. "I'll see you next month."

"That seems so far away."

"You got this."

"Thanks, Dr. Ellis."

"Take care of yourself, Joye."

Joye left that session feeling more vulnerable. She wasn't sure what she learned about herself or what was *fixed*. From her standpoint, all she had been doing was rehashing old stories from her past.

It took her a few days to address her assignment. She placed it on the nightstand, so she saw it when she went to bed and when she arose. She chose to ignore it and go on about her days and nights.

That night when she finally crawled into bed, she began to do the homework Dr. Ellis had assigned. It was rapid-fire as she completed the steps. Filled with determination, Joye reflected on one of the long-term relationships she hadn't mentioned during any of her sessions.

As she detailed them inside of her journal, she also relived them in her mind.

❧

Scrabble Man

The airport was crowded as usual that night. Joye was expecting to be picked up almost an hour prior by Elliott. When she told him that her flight from Chicago would land in Atlanta at 5:44 p.m., he promised he wouldn't be late. Well, in Joye's eyes "he lied" again because it was 7:19 p.m. according to her watch.

Elliott and Joye dated on and off for about five years. She was living in Atlanta, and he lived in Dallas where they were first introduced by her cousin in 2012. They started out long-distance like the majority of her relationships, but this one grew pretty quickly. Joye didn't seek out long-distance relationships, but they seemed to be what she attracted. She didn't think much of it until things got hard. Long-distance was not only difficult but also expensive to maintain. So Elliott decided to move to Atlanta; since he was a music producer, he had the flexibility and means to do so. Plus, they had been ring shopping, so an engagement was likely the next step if this relationship was to last. For Joye, it was the only logical next step with all of the breaking up and making up they had done over the years. But they agreed to live separately until they were married, so he rented a place not too far from her. Over time, they both acknowledged there were lots of things wrong with the relationship, but they tried not to focus on that and just work through it all. Joye had enough going on and he believed that relationships were supposed to be long-suffering. Unfortunately, her parents' example of marriage co-signed Elliott's beliefs, so they stick it out until death did them part.

At the airport, Joye wore her signature travel look: ragged jeans, a white t-shirt, and a baseball cap, and still looked cute.

Joye was serious about her comfortable travel wear—especially after such an exhausting trip from Chicago. To be clear, she wasn't always this rational when it came to travel gear. There was a time when she would travel in four-inch stilettos and wouldn't miss a beat leaving practicality in the wind.

Frustrated, Joye sat down across from baggage claim. She held her head in her hand then began to rub her temples as if she had a headache. She was fidgeting in her seat and looking around hoping to see her guy come through that door at any moment. She really couldn't believe Elliott was late.

There was a gentleman sitting in the seat next to her. He noticed how anxious she was. He tapped her quickly, yet gently on the shoulder, and said, "I think he's here." Joye followed his eyes across the room, and he was right. Elliott was walking briskly toward her with a stupid smirk on his face.

"What a welcome home." Joye rolled her eyes and stood up to grab her bag, but he grabbed her hand and pulled her close to him. He embraced her and said, "I'm sorry Boo." He sounded sincere, but Joye had already made up her mind that she was mad.

"Yeah, I know. But you're always late. I'm used to it. Don't like it, but I'm used to it." Joye was good at using sarcasm to mask her hurt and pain. At least that's what she thought, but her nonchalant, dismissive attitude was easy to see through.

"Let's get outta here before I get a ticket and end up in the Fulton County Jail," he said, as they walked to the car.

"It's Clayton County." Joye was correct, but her sarcasm was biting.

"Actually, I think we're both right but whatever. This is yo' city! Either way, I'm going to have to sit there for a couple of days 'cause you're cheap when it comes to me." He was trying hard to lighten the mood and make Joye smile.

"You damn right! You're my sugar daddy."

His attempt worked. Joye was happy to see him. She had been gone for two weeks since her father died of a massive heart attack. She and her sister, Melanie, flew to Chicago to help their mother with arrangements and settle his affairs. After dealing with funeral arrangements and other family business, Joye was tired and homesick, so that hour-long wait at the airport didn't help her mood at all.

Elliott wasn't able to make it to her father's funeral because he was out of town on business. Joye tried to be understanding, even though she wanted Elliott with her. She didn't make a big deal about it and just brushed it off as another non-issue that didn't need to be argued about.

Elliott loaded her bags into the back of his brand new 2017 Hummer H3 truck while Joye waited in the passenger seat. She watched him as he lifted all of her bags. She was glad he was able to be there for her at this moment. He was a good man. He had his share of issues, but still a good man. And he was hers, so she tried to deal with all of the things that came with him.

The drive to Joye's house was a little tense and somewhat awkward.

"How much shopping did you do?"

"Too much. I'm pretty sure I maxed out my credit card. I'll pay it off when I get settled back in." Embarrassed, she wanted to justify her actions. "It was very therapeutic. After Ma decided on everything, I was just over it and everybody in the family. Ya know? Everything was so last minute, so unexpected.

You know I hate to rush. Plus, being there for so long? Uh uh. Never again."

Elliott reached over and placed his hand on Joye's thigh. "Well, I'm sure you handled your business. You always do." Elliott was concerned about her, but he wasn't exactly sure of what to do or say. "You okay?" he asked gently.

"Yes. I'm okay. I'm dealing with it." Going against her initial thoughts to vent about the troubles of the trip, Joye instead focused on his absence and admitted to him that she wished he could have been there with her.

"Nah. I don't."

"What!?"

"Joye, you know I hate funerals. That stuff gives me the creeps, especially Black funerals: y'all like to have open caskets and shit. What the hell is that all about? I don't want to be looking at a dead body for hours. It's ridiculous."

"Wow. Really, Elliott? You think you can tell 'Asshole' to go away for just a second? I'm really not in the mood to talk to him right now."

"I'm sorry. I'm just not good with this kinda stuff. This whole consoling thing isn't one of my strong points. But you know that I'm here for you. Just say the word, and I got you."

"You suck at this consoling thing? Like, you're not good at it at all so just stop talking." Glossing over the issues, as usual, Joye leaned over and kissed him on the cheek to relieve the tension. She wanted him to know that she really didn't want to fight. At least, not tonight she didn't. "I'd just rather look at you anyway." Elliott smiled.

When they arrived at Joye's house, Joye was rambling through her bags and pockets trying to locate her keys. "Ugghhhhh! I can't find my keys."

"Baby, baby, don't worry. I have mine."

One morning when Joye sent him on a standard coffee run he decided to stop and get a duplicate key made. His intentions were to use it in circumstances such as this: Joye being away for an undetermined length of time and he'd be able to do something special for her. Joye was very meticulous about her space, so it was always work for her when she'd take extended trips away from home. Sometimes it was spoiled food in the fridge, sometimes it was smelly garbage hanging around. This time he would ensure that there was nothing for her to do other than come home, take a bath, and sleep.

Surprised, Joye scoffed "Mine what? I never gave you a key."

"I know. I made one before you left so I could come over and check on things since your return date was "undetermined." He gestured with air quotes.

"Well, my return date was undetermined because I didn't know how long it would take to bury my daddy!" Joye was clearly annoyed with his insinuation. "And, Elliott, what things did you think you needed to check up on?"

He smirked, "Things. Like everything. Just making sure the place was intact. Ya know, safe?"

"You are so fucking annoying. Give me my goddamn key, Elliott."

"I didn't know me looking out for you was such a big deal, girl." Almost enraged, Joye snatched the key from her beau. To her surprise when she opened her door her home was spotless. She had made a huge mess packing for her trip to Chicago, but it was no longer a mess thanks to Elliott.

Joye never really liked surprises. As a matter of fact, she hated them. Mostly because she's a little control freak but also because most people's idea of a surprise just didn't live up to her standards. While she didn't like the idea of Elliott having a "secret" key to her house, his intentions were pure. This was really the only way he knew how and felt comfortable showing up for her.

"Oh! You're welcome, baby." He said sarcastically.

Joye felt bad for snapping. "Oh my God, babe! You cleaned up?" She turned around and gently grabbed his face and gave him a few soft kisses all over his face.

"You're welcome. You're welcome. But you know I ain't clean up nothing. The cleaners had to deal with your dirty panties this time."

"First of all, you're not funny. And *FIRST* of all," Joye said again to make sure Elliott understood that all of her points were equally as important, "I don't have dirty panties!"

They laughed.

It was a sweet ending to a turbulent ride home. These were the moments when Joye realized things could never be perfect all the time and that she needed to enjoy the pieces of happiness, appreciation, and love received through her journey as they came. This would be especially true during times when she found it difficult to love, appreciate, and be happy within herself.

Even though she really wanted him to, Elliott didn't spend the night with Joye. He had other obligations and needed to catch a red-eye to Los Angeles for work, again. So the thirty-minute ride from the airport to her place, a shower, a little takeout, and a very quick, but much needed, lovemaking session was all the time Elliott had for her on this night. She didn't complain—this time.

Joye was never the type to get in the way of his work. She understood how erratic the music industry could be; not to mention the diva-like artists, but she desperately wanted him to put her first, if not all of the time, some of the time. She wanted him to make someone or something else wait instead of her for a change. Joye wanted to be his priority. Like many men who are ambitious and focused on their career trying to make money and provide for their family or for the life they envisioned, he found it difficult to make as much time for her as she requested.

He was consumed by his work and his work required him to travel often—sometimes at the drop of a dime. Joye was supportive, but she wasn't happy about it. In her mind, people always made time for things they were interested in. Dealing with Elliott, this meant she felt as if he was uninterested in her a lot of the time. But she loved him. This was the fee she had to pay for his love.

Her need for him was secondary to his everything. They'd make plans, he'd cancel because of a studio session or to take a last-minute meeting with some exec. Too often when they were together, he was distracted with work or trying to wind down from work while she was hoping to go out on dates or spend quality time together. His idea of quality time was being physically in her presence. Her idea of quality time was being present in each other's presence. Quite a difference. But she suffered through it without a word—most of the time.

One time while they were on vacation in Napa Valley, Joye assumed they both wanted to have some quiet time together.

After a long day of visiting vineyards, tasting wine, and sightseeing through the mountains she invited him into the bath when they returned to their hotel room. "Baby? You coming in?"

"No, babe. You enjoy it. I'll be here waiting for you." He barely even looked up from his phone. He was playing Scrabble. He must have been winning.

Joye was starting to feel insecure. Here she was this beautiful, sexual woman dying to let loose with her man, and he was more intrigued by playing a game. She had no choice other than to go to plan B. She bathed and put on a really sexy tiny red lace two-piece undergarment. Her signature go-to move. Maybe that would move his attention from his phone screen to her.

"Hey, you." She stood in the door of the bathroom for a second to see if he would notice how good she looked for him, but he didn't budge. Elliott just sat on the bed with his face buried in his phone. Joye crawled into the bed a little discouraged. It's hard to find the confidence to seduce a man who seems completely uninterested. But they were vacationing in wine country for Christ's sake, so why not try. It was supposed to be a fun and romantic trip but here she was laying on the bed trying to look sexy and get her man's attention. She rubbed on him, she kissed his neck and nibbled his ears a few times, she did everything but pull his dick out of his pants. Meanwhile, Elliott had turned into Scrabble Man and was spelling "organ" for fifty-eight points on his phone. It was quite clear; they weren't going to be using any of their *reproductive* organs that night. Feeling rejected, she put on her bathing suit and headed down to the pool.

Joye became second fiddle to not only work and the games on his phone, but she also took a back seat to the incessant calls and needs of his friends and clients.

One night while they were having dinner at Elliott's place before he headed out of town again, he interrupted their nice evening with another Elliott special--breaking his commitment to her by nonchalantly saying, "Babe? I'm not going to make it to your Christmas party this year." He scooped up a forkful of mashed potatoes and ate them. "Jeff's being presented with an award in Vegas on that same night, and since he's out of the country I have to accept it on his behalf," Elliott said then he guzzled a sip of his wine.

Rolling her eyes, "Ugh." Joye was a fixer, so she quickly offered a resolution, "Well, I can move my party, so I can go to the awards ceremony with you. I mean I move the date every year, so it's not a big deal. My friends won't be upset." Joye waited for a response but Elliott was chewing and dumping steak and potatoes into his mouth like it was his last supper. "Plus, I can be your award since you aren't getting one." She chuckled and tried to kill the tightness that was starting to fill up the air. Still no response from Elliott just yet. Joye continued to try to make things right, "I already have a dress so...boom! Problem-O! Solved-O!"

Finally, Elliott responded. "That would be nice, but I only have one ticket. Jeff already gave all the other seats at his table away." He knew Joye wouldn't be happy, so he tried to cover the facts quickly and get out of this conversation unscathed.

Not believing a word he said, Joye lost her appetite. She stood up from the kitchen table, picked up her plate, and emptied it down the garbage disposal. As she began rinsing her plate off, she rebutted, "Well maybe we can buy another ticket?"

"Nope. They sold out." He realized his nope was inappropriately too harsh and too quick. Now he was trying to clean things up. He abruptly got up from the table, walked over to her, and grabbed her around the waist pulling her closer to him. "Buutttt, I'll ask around and see if anyone cancels or has an extra ticket that I can grab for you. Is that okay?"

"El? You know I really hate this. You always end up canceling on me."

"I know. I'm sorry. It'll just be a few days. I think I'm traveling Tuesday night and back on Thursday. We can get together and do something nice then. Okay?"

Elliott always thought he could make up for his disappointments by scheduling another date and time for them to get together. At this point, Joye was tired of being let down. His attempts to reschedule meant nothing because his reschedules had to be rescheduled.

She didn't argue before, but she argued that night. Joye moved Elliott's hand from around her waist and stepped away from him.

"No! Did you tell him you had other plans already? Or did you just say 'yes' like a good boy and basically 'fuck me'?" It was clear that Joye had already taken it too far before the argument could get off the ground.

Elliott kept his cool but was not in the mood for a fight. "Don't start. We've been doing this for too long for you to start acting like you don't know what's going on. This is how I can afford to take you on vacation, pay bills, buy you jewelry, take you shopping...Don't start complaining about this shit now because you can't get your way."

"That's what you think this is?" Joye yelled. "I don't give a fuck about none of that stupid shit you just said." By this time,

Joye was furious and began pacing up and down the floor. She wanted to slap the shit out of him, but she was only violent in her mind. However, her words could be lethal, and she was far from finished with this conversation. "And I damn sure ain't trying to get my way," she continued. "I never get my way. Let's be crystal fucking clear about that." In her mind, Joye added the word "bitch," at the end of that sentence, but she didn't say it.

"Are you finished?" he asked.

"Naw! We had plans. PLANS!" Joyed yelled with emphasis insinuating that he didn't know the definition of the word. "Do you know what plans are? A fucking commitment that once again you so easily broke without the common fucking courtesy of telling me before you agreed to go changing shit around!" Joye plopped down on the chair.

Elliott was staring at her little performance unbothered. "So you're gonna filibuster this argument? Okay. Go 'head."

Joye peered at him. "Yes, you stupid asshole. I'm going to filibuster this fucking argument because you ain't never got shit to say after you fuck everything up. I'm just supposed to take it, right?" She stood up and took a step towards him while flailing her hands around. Somehow, she thought that made her argument more poignant. "Then you wanna throw money in my face like I fucking need your money! I don't need your money. But that's your response for everything! Money. Ugh. Any nigga can buy me things. Stop putting your value on how much money you spend in this relationship! That's not all you are required to do."

"Oh, any nigga? Really? Oh, okay. I'm out." Elliott headed to his bedroom and grabbed his duffle bag.

"Classic. Yeah, you're out. I know. You had to create an argument with me before you leave so you can get your little three or four-day break to do what you really want to do. Yeah, bye! "

"Let any nigga do that shit while I'm in Vegas, WORKING." Elliott wanted to make it clear to Joye that what he wanted to do was work and that anything else implied was her own insecurities talking.

They had been having major disagreements about work all the time lately. Elliott loved Joye in his own special way. He didn't want to lose her, but he definitely wasn't ready to do any of the things that she wanted to feel solid in their relationship. He literally just wanted her to shut the fuck up, orgasm as soon as he penetrated her, and allow him to do things however he wanted--right or wrong. No questions asked. Just fuck him and shut the fuck up except when fucking him, then she could talk again. Those were his words.

"I'll see you when I get back," Elliott said as he walked out of the house.

"Whatever. I can't stand your dumb ass."

This was their relationship dynamic. For years, they spent a lot of time breaking up and making up. As if his broken promises time and time again wasn't enough, eventually his desire for other women took on a life of its own.

Even though Joye was more than enough for Elliott, it was much easier for him to grab a girl on the road or fall back into a pattern that was comfortable and easy for him. No expectations or requirements. No accountability. Just sex.

Joye and Elliott had invested so much time in each other. They did their best to be there for each other, but Elliott wanted and demanded a version of Joye that she didn't feel he deserved.

Joye felt that he only gave a portion of himself while she was all in. Joye was tired of failing. She had given what she thought was everything she had to sustain her relationship with Elliott including her time, her space, her love, her knowledge, support, and understanding with him. After a while, though, all she was sharing was her rage, resentment, and foul mouth.

Was he enough for her?

Maybe.

His friends loved Joye and told him that she was perfect for him.

Her friends were riding with whatever choice she made and not saying anything against it. It wasn't until she proclaimed that she was truly done with him that some of her loved ones expressed their disdain and belief that she was settling in a major way. They liked him; they just didn't like him for her.

Joye had to learn her own lessons and grow into the decision of finding and getting her worth on her own, but it was through an exhaustive process. Everything she already knew, every red flag she continued to ignore, every reason she designed in her mind about the investment into this relationship as a reason to stick it out, all came crashing down. Elliott being there for her after her father died only made her feel more guilty and obligated to trying to work at her miserable relationship.

Eventually, Joye decided that she wanted more, and she was going to figure out a way to get just that.

So finally, after five years, she walked away.

As she sat alone for the first time in years, reflecting on her past, it triggered her to reminisce about a pivotal moment she shared with her dad before he died.

The Father of Lies

Joye ran up the stairs into her dad's sitting area. This is where he loved to watch TV, listen to music, and water his plants. *Family Feud* was showing, but the sound was muted. Mary J. Blige's "I'm Going Down," was playing on the stereo, but it eventually skipped to Nancy Wilson, "The Good Life." Nancy was much more his speed even though he did like to cut a groove every now and again, especially in his younger days.

Mr. Allyn was watering the plants and humming to the music. The aging process was catching up to him, so he was moving slower than he was the last time she had seen him. Watching him age was sweet, yet painful for Joye and her sister.

"Daddy, do you think I have a fear of commitment?" Joye said immediately upon seeing her father.

Mr. Allyn was a little startled but didn't miss a beat moving on to the next plant. "Hell no. Little girl, you don't seem to be afraid of nothing. The way you run all around the world by yourself. How could that be fear?"

"I mean with—"

Mr. Allyn interrupted Joye and gave a sharp look. "Are you going to say good morning? You just walk in my house and start blabbin' out the mouth? You definitely get that from yo mama." Mr. Allyn shook his head as he finished watering his plants then sat down in his big chair.

"Ugh. Good morning, Daddy. I said good morning to Mom when I walked in so I—"

"So you thought I didn't need to hear it for myself? You know I never understood that about you kids. If y'all say something to me it's my job to tell your mother. If y'all tell her something she's supposed to tell it to me." Mr. Allyn shook his head repeatedly. "You'd think by now with all those degrees we've been paying for that you and your sister would know that it doesn't work like that."

"Well, it ain't our fault that you and Mom don't know how to communicate properly." Joye was always a smart aleck.

"Watch your mouth, now. And you got your damn nerves talking about proper communication when you just ran up here with words spilling out of your mouth. I know if I didn't raise you well enough to have common courtesy, your mama certainly did."

Joye wasn't expecting her father to check her like that. "Yes, y'all did. Sorry, Pop."

"Umm hmm. Now, what are you trying to ask me?" He motioned for Joye to sit down on the chair across from him.

"Oh," Joye plopped on the chair and folded her leg under her like she was an 8-year-old kid. "I was asking if you think I have a fear of commitment. Like in a relationship. Do you think I'm afraid to share my life with someone?"

Mr. Allyn took a deep breath and clenched his hands together as he thought about his response. "You may be afraid to share your space. You know how you act up when someone messes up your stuff?" They were both chuckling because it was true. Joye did not like people touching her things.

"I just like cleanliness and order, Daddy. And I got some of that from you, so cut it out."

"Are you trying to tell me something? Should I be pulling out my blue suit?" He joked.

"Oh, God. No. Keep your little raggedy suit in the closet."

Mr. Allyn got a little more serious. "Why are you asking me

about this commitment stuff?"

"I just want to know what you think."

"Well, I've seen you commit to a lot of things and do really well. But if you want me to be honest, you've never brought a boy around so I guess I would say 'yes' unless you like girls and that's okay too."

"Daddy. I don't like girls. And you need to stop saying that to Melanie because she is a whole fool."

"She's still teasing you about that?"

"Of course she is, Daddy! Nonstop. She's so annoying."

Mr. Allyn was looking around for something, "Well, that's your baby sister. She just wants you to be happy."

"What are you looking for, Daddy? The remote?" Joye got up and grabbed the remote from the top of the television and handed it to him.

"Oh, yeah. Thanks, baby." Mr. Allyn began scrolling through channels.

Joye continued, "You know, Melanie just wants me to have a corny husband like her."

Mr. Allyn looked over at Joye and said, "He is kinda corny." They both laughed. Mr. Allyn finally stopped changing the channel, sat the remote down, and turned his full attention to Joye. "Again, what's up with all this commitment talk? You ready to settle down with someone?"

"Not now, but eventually. I definitely want a husband one day."

"Well, you gotta date someone first, honey. When are you going to start dating someone?"

"I *have* dated someone."

"Well, why haven't you brought him here so me and your

mama can check him out and give you our blessing?"

"Well, that's kinda why I'm asking the question, Daddy. By the time we get to the point where I am ready for them to meet you and Ma, they seem to pull away. I was thinking maybe it's me and not them with the problem."

"Aww, ain't nothing wrong with you, girl. Men just get cold feet sometimes." Mr. Allyn stood up from his chair and slowly walked over to the window. "Come here and look at this." Mr. Allyn pointed to the area where he had several of the same types of plants. "These are your favorite flowers, right?" He asked.

"Yep. Orchids."

"Do you know it takes 6 to 8 months for these things to mature? Takes 3 months to flower and they'll bloom beautifully for months, then they just die. Or, at least they appear to die only to re-bloom again in 8 to 12 months. It just depends. Each one is different. Some never re-bloom. And they all almost always operate on their own schedule even though I water them with the same amount of water and make sure they have the same amount of sunlight and humidity levels at the same time." Mr. Allyn turned to Joye and put his arm around her shoulder. "You know men are like your favorite flower? You have to be patient. This stuff takes time. Don't be so hard on yourself or them." He patted Joye on the back and walked back to his chair and sat down. "And let them be the man. Stop being so damn independent all the time. You can't do everything by yourself."

"I'm only independent because I don't have anyone to do things for me," Joye said. She was fighting back her tears, so she dropped her head and walked back to her seat even though she desperately wanted her father to just give her a big hug.

"And when I step back," she continued, "they don't step forward to handle their business, so I end up having to do it all anyway." Joye let out an exasperated sigh and looked at her father. "Like why do I need you if I still have to do your job when you're around?"

"Sounds like you're looking for Mr. Perfect," he said, as he peered over the rims of glasses at Joye.

"Wow, really? I thought I was asking for Mr. Basic." She shrugged.

Mr. Allyn leaned forward in his chair and rubbed his index finger across his chin. "Listen, I wish I could have shown you and your sister a better example of a father and a husband when you were younger. I know you still have it in the back of your mind that your mom is unhappy, and I am a terrible person. But what matters is me and your mother figured it out and we are still here together. She's getting all the attention I didn't give her for 30 years." Mr. Allyn sounded remorseful for what he considered his failures as a father and husband but that didn't last long. "But now she's got something new to complain about! So this complaining you're doing you're going to keep doing because you're a woman and that's what y'all do. And, you know what, if you girls lived here instead of down South, I would be able to be more active in your lives. Then maybe y'all will really forgive me for being gone so much when y'all were growing up."

Annoyed that her father always found a way to blame everyone else but himself, Joye responded. "Daddy, we've had planes since 1903. We've invited you down and sent for you several times. You just don't want to come. So, we come see you." She made a face at her father but was trying to not be disrespectful. "That's kinda the same in my relationships. It's like I have to do all the work to get a piece of them."

"Maybe you should ask your mom. She's probably a lot better at discussing these things." Mr. Allyn picked up the remote control again. Instead of flipping through the channels, he turned up the volume. He was done with the conversation because it was shifting to an uncomfortable place and becoming about him. Joye kissed him on the cheek. She had to get to the airport and fly back to Atlanta in a few hours.

"Oh, Daddy? When I do have *something* to tell you. I will also be buying you a new suit because that blue one is out of style, playa!" Joye didn't want to leave her father with that awkward and uncomfortable feeling so she reverted back to her humor.

"Y'all better not touch my damn suit," Mr. Allyn snapped.

"I'm gonna tell mom to burn it. Love you."

"I love you too. When are you coming back?"

Joye shouted as she ran down the stairs, "Soon!" She kissed and hugged her mom on her way out the door and left.

On her flight she was thinking about what her father said to her earlier. She was thinking about being the one taking the steps toward him to keep the relationship intact. It was eerily similar to how she behaved in her intimate relationships. Joye was beginning to feel burnt out. She was giving too much all of the time, and she didn't know how to stop. She believed that if she stopped then the relationships would end. If she didn't reach out to her father and go visit him then she would not see him. This was her attitude about many things in life: If I don't do it, it won't get done.

Dr. Ellis had been pushing Joye to discuss her intimate relationships and find through lines within each of them. She wanted Joye to discover the repetitive behaviors and patterns in her relationships and really understand how love was showing up in her life: from the airports, the long-distance, the emotional distance, poor communication, being last on the list, all the way down to the sex.

Joye compared her men to her father. She thought she could compensate for the things she missed in him. Joye wanted to be loved, protected, provided for, and understood but she was having a hard time. She saw her lovers as semblances of Mr. Allyn. She told Dr. Ellis that they were selfish men or greedy men with no consideration of what a partner was or what she needed in the relationship. The hurt she felt from feeling invisible at times, to fighting her battles alone, was really eating her up.

She just wanted one answer: Why?

ॐ

all the queen's [ME]n

Finding [ME] in Men

I kept choosing the same man over and over again hoping he'd love me differently than the last. Maybe this time he would love me better or stronger or with more passion. Maybe the next love would be longer, real-er, and more satisfying in every way. But it wasn't happening. I was getting something but never all I wanted in one take.

I kept wondering what in the hell is wrong with men. I needed to have a chat with God or the Universe about why men are wired the way they are because I really wanted and needed to understand.

What am I missing?

You'd think with all the experience I had with the opposite sex that I would know way more about what men desired, needed, thought, or felt.

People say treat others how you want to be treated, give the kind of love that you want to receive, and insisted that you get what you give, right? But that's not my story. I get a glimpse of what I want early on in the relationships then it would fade away. If I ask too many questions, if I demand to be treated with respect, if I stand up for myself in any way, I become the enemy. Instead of realizing that I was dealing with compounded pain I chose to focus on the flaws of the person. Whenever one of them would pull further and further away from me I needed to come up with reasons why that didn't include me. So I began convincing myself that they weren't man enough, they weren't ready, their mommas didn't raise them right, they didn't have decent male friends or a father to put them on code and tell them they were wrong!

Happy wife (or woman, girlfriend, or fiancé), happy life.

Most of the time it feels to me as if none of my men really cared about my happiness.

Why do I keep choosing these selfish ass men?

My love life is turning into a tragedy. I am losing control of what I used to think made me powerful. And now I was laying on a therapist's couch trying to work it out. I am proud of this step though.

I wasn't always holding myself accountable for my choices in the way I knew I should.

I am trying though.

It just felt like I was the only one trying in the relationships so often that it was easier to put the focus on the other person. The reality is I was connecting physically, but I still wasn't doing enough to support their needs outside of the bedroom. And, by my recollection, I was missing a few key marks inside the bedroom too.

I was moving in and out of relationships thinking that the next time it will be better because I was better. So I thought. At best, I was just a little more aware. Being aware was only one part of the solution. Once awareness kicks in I needed to correct myself.

Even though I am feeling out of control the power was always within me to choose. I just want so desperately to be understood.

To be chosen

To be first on someone's list of things to do.

Through it all, I am beginning to learn that I was asking these men to give me something that I wasn't even giving myself.

When I was growing up, my father was a workaholic, so I didn't get to see him or spend that much time with him. We had a big family filled with aunts and uncles, nieces and nephews, so our house was filled with people during holidays, birthdays, and graduations. My parents made sure our house was available to the family especially in times of need. I think there was too much going on all the time for anyone to recognize that daddy wasn't really tuned into our day-to-day lives at home. Hell, I didn't even realize it until I started looking at my relationships and relating them to my daddy issues. The lack of my father's presence in the household should have been considered the first toxic male interaction but it was not. Not in my eyes. I gave that title to the scumbag teacher who was copping feels under the desk during work-study and tutoring or while I stood in the lunch line. Or when he'd ask me to stay behind and help with a "special project".

I never wanted to carry the victim torch which is interesting considering I have absolutely been victimized by many, many people. My outlook on life, the ability to sort through the trauma and still remain a picture – perfect image of positivity and optimism could easily be the result of all the trauma I've endured. It essentially has become my coping mechanism.

My motto for pain is "You got 30 minutes to wallow in it and then move on. We got shit to do."

That worked for me for a long time. Turning forty showed me that that tactic wasn't going to be as easy as it was in my younger days. My mind and body simply wouldn't allow the quick pass easy way out of my pain. After 40, I had to sit in it and sort it out properly in order to move on.

This is me trying to sort it out.

The thing that was missing in all of these relationships was me. I was completely invisible to them and to myself. I had to see myself. I had to choose myself first. I had to understand and love myself. I had to make myself a priority, but I had the gall to ask someone to do it for me though.

This was my daddy issue spilling over into my adult life. His apology lifted a heavy weight, but it was no fix.

There is still much work to do

I'm working on it.

fami[LIAR]
dick

> *"If you consider a woman less pure after you've touched her, maybe you should take a look at your hands."*
>
> - KAIJA SABBAH

The Boring Barber

Joye called Terry.

She was still bruised by the young guy wasting her time and being alone was not helping her feel any better.

"It's nice to hear from you. To what do I owe the pleasure?" Terry was excited to get a call from her.

Pressing her own agenda Joye probed, "What are you up to?"

"Oh, just working out...doing some work in the yard. Lounging around. What are you up to?"

Joye wasn't truly interested in his day; she just wanted to come over. "Just finished shopping. You want some company?"

"Tonight? Sure!" He loved how direct Joye could be at times.

Terry was an easy ask because Joye knew that he wasn't dating anyone and that his lifestyle generally was spent at home. The odds of him saying yes were in her favor. "Okay. I'll be there tonight at 8. Is that cool?"

"Yes, ma'am. I'll cook dinner." Done.

Just that like, Joye made an old school booty call with an ex that she wasn't really into, but he had the penis, and he was available. He was handsome. He wasn't too far. He was safe, and he enjoyed her when she came around. That was all Joye needed to scratch the itch. It was that simple for her with this guy.

She never got her hopes up with him though. They dated for a little while back in the day. Terry looked good on paper, and for Joye, the idea of what they could be together versus who she and Terry were separately is what mattered most. He was tall, studious and strait-laced and she fit the perfect imagery of a trophy wife. A perfect disaster.

When Joye arrived at 8 o'clock sharp she was clear about why she was there. He, on the other hand, was hopeful and salivating like a little puppy. Terry knew the routine though because it had been going on for several years. Joye went from "I think I met my husband" to "just take off your pants."

He greeted Joye at the door with a wine glass filled with one of her favorites: Cabernet Sauvignon. "Hi, Sexy." He was very tall, so he had to lean down to kiss Joye on her cheek.

This was new for him.

Terry was lazy, so he typically unlocked his door and let her find him on the couch waiting for her.

"Oooh. This is nice. Thank you."

"A cabernet for the lady."

"Ahh. You remembered."

"And I won't ever forget," he said while looking around for her overnight bag. "Do you need me to get anything from the car?"

"Nope. It's just me."

"Cool. I hope you brought your appetite tonight because your boy threw down in the kitchen once again."

Chuckling, "Oh, Lord. You swear you're Emeril! What did you make?"

He had gotten playful and was bippity bopping around Joye. "That's how you see me? Like the old fat Italian? I'm more like G. Garvin sweetie. Black and bald." He lightly smacked Joye on her butt. "Just go wash your hands and meet me in the dining room young lady."

Joye wasn't used to him taking charge or being aggressive, so she was a little fascinated by this behavior. She gladly did as she was told.

His house was big and beautiful, though it wasn't well decorated. It was as if he had bought the house he intended to have for his wife and children but moved his bachelor pad furniture in. Well, except the bed. The bed was on some grown ass man status. Terry had custom ordered a "family size" bed that was 12 feet by 6 feet. It was a navy suede platform bed with a paneled headboard that reached the top of his 12-foot ceilings and spanned across the entire wall. The bedding was the same blue as the bed, but he had a few ivory and gold throw pillows and a rustic cowhide spot throw perfectly laid across the corner of the bed. It was massive; it was beautiful; it was fit for a king.

Terry also had nice kitchen pots. He loved to cook, so he invested pretty heavily in the kitchen.

Joye walked into the dining room and was a little shocked. She was expecting the usual. You know? A plated dinner of chicken or salmon or steak, potatoes or rice, asparagus or a salad, and bread and butter *at* the table. But he had set up the perfect indoor picnic on the floor. He had laid down multiple blankets and topped them with oversized pillows. There was a large rectangular glass in the center of the layout with white candles flickering all around. He accented the centerpiece with a beautiful array of fresh peach and white roses and Gerbera daisies, orange lilies and carnations, and some plush greenery. There was chocolate-covered fruit, an epic charcuterie board, a bottle of wine, and a picnic basket with food in it. It looked like something made for a Greek Goddess. Miles Davis' "Blue in Green" was beginning to fade out and "I Want You" by Marvin Gaye began to play.

Joye felt special. A feeling she loved to feel and craved from her man. "Okay playlist. Wow. What did you do?"

"Well, I've been wanting to do something like this for a while. When you called you gave me a good reason. Do you like it?" He was happy that she was happy with his work. He was thinking that tonight could be the night that he did enough to spark a real relationship between them.

"No, I hate it!" Joye joked. "Of course, I love it. This is beautiful. You did this by yourself? Who did you pay? You should give them a big fat tip."

"Nope. I did this all by myself. And Google and YouTube gave me a few ideas. But I'm glad you like it." He grabbed her hand and helped her sit down on what is commonly known in the South as "a pallet of blankets." When she got situated, he looked her in her eyes, and mannishly announced, "Oh, by the way, you're the only one getting a big fat tip tonight."

"Touché. This earned you a new trick tonight."

"Oh, I'm getting tricks tonight? Okay. I didn't know. Thank you. Thank you very much."

"You're welcome very much."

Joye was enthralled with the energy of newness he was giving off. At this moment she was thinking maybe he wasn't boring after all. Clearly, he knew how to take initiative, and maybe, just maybe, this could turn into something more and he was indeed the husband she thought she met several years back.

"So what did you throw down on, boy? I'm starving."

"Let's see." He opened the picnic basket and began laying out the food.

"Sandwiches? Chicken? Fried chicken?! I thought you said you threw down in the kitchen?"

"I did. On the decor. Are you hungry or not?" Joye nodded yes. "Then let's eat," he said.

As nice as the setup and introduction to dinner was it only turned out to be an okay evening. They laughed a lot; mostly because Joye was cracking sarcastic jokes. And, because he put so much emphasis on decor the food was basic at best. But she chewed with a grin and pretended to have a good time. She was ready for this part to be over and get what she came for.

Thirty-minutes in, Joye abruptly said, "I'm tired."

"Okay. You wanna head upstairs and I'll straighten up this mess?"

"I'll help you clean—."

"No. I got it. Go upstairs. I'll be there in a few minutes. You know where everything is, so help yourself to whatever you need."

Walking up the stairs Joye was thinking she would get her fix and go but when she walked through his bedroom and opened the door to his master bathroom, she was reminded of how accommodating he had been this entire night. He laid out white towels--because he remembered that is the only color towels she would use, her favorite soap--L'Occitane Shea Butter Extra Gentle Soap - Verbena and matching lotion and all of the toiletries she would need like Q-tips, makeup remover wipes, a fresh toothbrush, and a brand new loofah. He placed a bouquet of a dozen long stem red roses and a red gift box with beautiful emerald green lace panties and camisole in it on the bathtub. There was also a small card. It read:

J,

A beautiful woman deserves to be taken care of.

It was no secret that Joye wanted to be lavished by the man in her life. She was a sucker for sweet gestures. Receiving gifts was definitely her love language but so was physical touch.

She showered and put on her sexy little lingerie pieces. She was hopeful that the great start and fresh edge he had at the unfolding of the night would extend through his typical mechanical lovemaking techniques. She was also hoping he would take off his white sweat socks before he got in the bed and touched her.

Wishful thinking. When she opened the doors to step into

the bedroom, there he was sprawled across the bed in his boxers and his socks scrolling through his cell phone.

"Uh, uh! Those socks. You had me put this sexy ass lingerie
on and that's what you're gonna give me?"

"Just get over here." He put the phone down and reached
up and grabbed Joye's hand pulling her onto the bed. "You
look great."

"Thank you. It's really pretty and you got the si-" He hushed
her and kissed her hard on her mouth. They tangoed around
the bed for a little while. He was not a foreplay kind of guy, and
Joye was becoming more and more displeased with whatever
it was he was trying to do.

"Can you just put it in now?" She politely requested. And
for a few minutes, or less, he flipped her around, back and forth,
and talked a little bit asking her 'if she liked it'; She lied and said
'yeah'. He was panting and telling her how good she looked and
felt. Then it was over. He came, and Joye went to the bathroom
to clean herself up. She yelled over the water, "Do you want a
towel?" and he said no, that he was good. She thought, *Good!
You don't deserve hot towel treatment anyway!* She got back in
the bed. He had already comfortably placed himself under the
covers. She was annoyed by his performance, but she felt like
he owed her a little more dick...at least long enough where she
could help him get herself off. But then she heard snoring.

"Did this muthafucka really fall asleep like he put in some
work?!" She scoffed under her breath and shook her head.

Joye slipped off her panties, quickly pulled the cami off
over her head, and decided to sleep naked. She pushed her
body as close to his without waking him up and nestled there
for the rest of the night. When she woke up, she realized that

the *toot-that-thang-up-mommy-make-it-roll* technique did not work on him.

She had an attitude.

She didn't say good morning.

She didn't wash her face.

She didn't brush her teeth.

She put on her clothes and said goodbye with a fake smile and cold body language.

For the first time, Joye had awakened with a feeling of sexual discontent after having a consensual encounter.

She was frustrated and annoyed. She didn't want to make him feel bad despite the fact that he didn't make her feel good. So she would lie to herself and justify spending the night with her ex by saying it wasn't safe for her to drive home alone late at night. The truth was, his bed was comfortable; she was hopeful she could get more from him, and she was lazy. Whatever she had to say to convince herself of her decision, that nice bed didn't make up for the middle-of-the-road sex.

Joye hadn't been sexually active with anyone for several months after her stint with Jamel. This wasn't unusual for her. She would have these little escapades with guys and these abrupt breakups and then abstain from sex for a few months to "cleanse her body." She was a bit meticulous about her hygiene and way too egotistical to allow for any mishaps. She would never place herself in a position where she was confused about who the father of any potential pregnancy might be. Images of men breakdancing and pop-locking chanting 'I ain't da daddy!' on *Maury Povich* was more than enough for her to keep enough space between each dick appointment, but it must have been a full moon that night.

Instead of appropriately communicating what was wrong with her like an adult, she held it in and ran away. Apparently, there is nothing worse than wanting sex, getting sex, and the sex ending terribly.

She knew the sex was mediocre at best before she got there. So this was no one's fault but her own. Yet, because she wanted male attention and she needed some physical interaction to help soothe her pain, she overlooked her bad decision and made everything his fault because he couldn't deliver.

The Other Frat

As Joye walked herself to her car the phone rang. She had a Kool-Aid smile when she saw Bryce's name and number pop up on her phone screen.

"Good morning, Sir!"

"Hey, girl. What you got going today?"

This sounded like a familiar start to a conversation. "Nothing. Just chillin'. What about you?"

"I was just seeing if you wanted to come hang out with your boy." Hang out equaled code for have sex. Joye looked at the time and started calculating the hours from when she had sex with Terry to when she might see Bryce. She stuck up her nose at the idea that she was even entertaining this thought but was also looking for an excuse to do it.

"What time are you talking?"

"Like in a couple of hours."

"Oh. Okay. I have a little more running around to do. I'd need to go home and get cleaned up and then I can call you when I'm heading your way. I mean, it won't be quick."

"Nah, that's cool. I'm not going anywhere. If I do it will just be to the store or something. So, yeah, just give me a call when you get on the road."

What in the hell did she just do?

Talking out loud to herself, Joye battled with herself.

"You are out of control, ma'am!

"Men do this shit all the time.

"But they have outies. You have an innie.

"Ugh.

"This is gross.

"Well, I can just soak in the tub and douche.

"No. Douches are disgusting and cause infections.

"I, mean, we used a condom and I know I'll use one later on too so that should be okay, right?

"What the hell?

"If I space it out at least ten to twelve hours that should be fine.

"Hmmm?

"Do I count from the time it went in or from the time it came out??

"Oh, God.

"I need to call a hoe. I don't know any of these rules.

"Just call him and cancel.

"Yeah, yeah. Just call him and cancel."

But she didn't call Bryce and cancel. Instead, she got cleaned up and by the end of the night, she was headed to his house to "hang out" with him. And as she expected, he gave her all of the compliments and attention she was missing. Bryce turned off the TV. He didn't have his face in his phone all night. He gave her just what she was craving. He served her drinks from his bar and ordered take-out when she said she was hungry. He was affectionate with his words, his touch, and his kisses. She felt desired. They talked, laughed, and caught up on each other's life. No fancy gifts, no extravagant decor, just a good time with someone who knew how to zone in on her and how to satisfy her in the bedroom or on the couch or wherever.

That was enough for Joye, tonight.

Bryce invited Joye to spend the night and she accepted. She slept like a baby until he woke up in the middle of the night rock hard, poking and prodding. It was time for round two. They were up and at it throughout the night. By the time morning came, so had she—four times.

Now, she was full.

Joye began rustling around the covers looking for her underwear.

"You sure you can't stay for breakfast?"

"Is breakfast a new code for sex?"

Bryce looked at Joye like she was smoking crack. "Oh!" Joye said, "you mean, breakfast, breakfast? Wow.

When did we get to breakfast status?"

"If you want to get breakfast, we can get breakfast is all I'm saying."

"Oh. So, are you ready now?" Bryce had always told Joye that he wasn't interested in anything serious. Casual dating was his jam. Joye was confused by his request for her to stay for breakfast. She had spent plenty of nights with him over the years, but the next morning she would leave, and he'd be putting his sheets in the washer.

"I am ready to talk about it...with you."

"Really?"

"Joye? What's up? You can say no. I'd prefer a yes, but you know?"

"I know. I-I-Ii-I'm just surprised. I wasn't expecting that. I'm sorry."

"So yes or no? Breakfast with ya boy?"

"You gon' make me do the walk of shame into a cafe this morning?"

"Yep!" Bryce jumped up and slow trotted to his laundry room. "But I put your things in the washer when you were slobbering on my pillow last night. So technically, it ain't the walk of shame if your shit's clean." Bryce handed Joye her clothes.

"Is it dry? Aww, man. You got me. Okay. Put the gun down. Let's get breakfast."

"Cool."

They dressed and went to Urban Grind for coffee and their gourmet grilled cheese. The conversation was interesting. Bryce had a bit of a health scare a few months ago that set him on a new path. He was thinking about getting older, raising a family, and creating a legacy. With no children, he was working hard for nobody. His fear of settling down was being replaced with the fear of being alone; mostly, sick and alone.

"I'm not asking you to marry me tomorrow or anything like that. But if I'm going to choose someone today, it's you. And that's real shit. So..." Bryce put all of his cards on the table.

"Your honesty has always been such a turn on. I just appreciate it so much."

"You deserve it."

"Yes, I do."

"I'm feeling really rejected right now. You haven't even implied if you want to think about it or if you want to say no...you just curvin' ya boy!"

Laughing, "No I am not! I'm really just shocked. And—"

"Joye?" A female voice called out. They both looked up to be greeted by Ro.

Ro had a bright glowing brown skin with a pretty baby-face. No blemishes. No combination skin. She had perfect big, tight, and curly, natural hair. Perfect eyebrows. Perfect eyelashes. Perfect shaped eyes and lips. She was just a really pretty girl who seemed 20 years younger than she actually was. She was a little taller than Joye, but she would be considered about 15 pounds overweight for her height. Black men would call her slim thick. Magazines would call her curvy. She was fashionable all the time, even for an early Saturday morning coffee run. She never wore a lot of makeup because she didn't need it. And she always presented herself with the confidence of a woman on a mission.

"Heyyy! What are you doing on my side of town this early?" Joye asked Ro. Ro lived north of Atlanta and getting her to midtown or downtown was like pulling teeth.

"Oh my God. I accidentally had something shipped to my corporate office like a do-do. I wasn't trying to fool with FedEx's shady asses and have them attempt to reroute it, so the security guard held it for me so I could grab it today." Pulling out a chair to sit with them, Ro asked, "Y'all mind?"

"Not at all." Bryce said as he stood up to greet Ro. It had been over a year since he had seen Ro at a little get together Joye had at Kat's Cafe to celebrate one of her birthdays.

"Hey, girl, how you been?"

Ro was side-eyeing Joye with a face of confusion as he hugged her, "I'm good. How have *you* been?"

"Can't complain." Bryce decided this was a perfect time to leave this conversation that Joye seemed to be dodging. "So, listen. Imma head out."

"No!" Joye called out very girlishly. But he insisted.

"Think about what I said? Okay?"

"Yes. Absolutely. I will call you."

"Cool. You got your keys, right?"

"Yep. You wanna drive the car back to your house? I can get Ro to drop me to you..."

"Nope. I could use the walk." Bryce gave Joye a kiss on the mouth, all tongue before he walked out. Ro was staring with big eyes filled with a hundred questions. "Be good." He acknowledged Ro as he prepared to walk towards the exit, "It was good seeing you."

"You too."

Ro looked at Joye like "what in theeeee entire fuck is going on?" Joye put her head down and shook it side to side.

"What is happening right now? How are you over here with him? I'm pretty sure when I spoke to you last you were headed to Terry's house on the other side of town." Waiting for an explanation, she stared at her friend with bucked eyes.

"I was headed to his house."

"Aaand? You decided not to go?"

"Can I tell the story, Officer? Sheesh." Joye let out a huge sigh.

"Oh, this is about to be some bullshit."

"Shut up. So, I did go to Terry's house. It started off super nice too. He greeted me at the door with a glass of wine, he had a sexy ass indoor picnic set up in the kitchen. He—"

"In the kitchen? What happened to his table?"

"Bitch? He bought a new one. It hasn't been delivered yet. You gonna let me tell the story?"

"I got questions! Alright, go ahead." Ro took the first sip of her coffee. She curled up her nose and began to add sugar to it as she listened to Joye.

"He had candles and you know; it was really well thought out and nicely executed. I told him I thought he had paid someone to do it, but he said he did it all by himself. So, as usual, the conversation was dry. My hoo-hah was dry."

Ro interrupted, "Your hoo-hah was dry!? I cannot."

"Well, I was!" They both let out soft laughs. "Like, C'mon. I came here for one thing. So I hurry dinner along and begin making my way upstairs. Terry says get comfortable and he'll meet me up there. I head into the bathroom and he has roses spread out and a freakin' gift for me."

"A gift! What?"

"Yes, a gift. With a card that read 'You deserve to be taken care of.' And I'm like, 'whoa.'

"We are talking about Ter—?"

"Yes! Him. Trust me. I, too, was like 'who art thou?' So let me finish. Let me finish! Beautiful lingerie is the gift. So, I shower, whatever...and put it on." Joye dropped her voice a few octaves, gave Ro a look of disappointment, and asked her. "Do you want to play the disaster music now or later?"

"Wait," Ro asked the cashier for another cup of coffee. "Girl, what happened?"

"So, I comes out the bafroom," Joye begins in an awful New York accent. She had her right fist balled up and began pounding it into her left hand with every other word. "Boom! Check it. Ya mans is in his draws wit his socks on yo! So, I'm like, bet." Joye is clapping her hands and moving around in her seat like she's in a battle rap cypher. "Yo son! Take ya socks off!" They both are laughing way too loud to be sharing space in a public venue.

"Sssshhh. Stop being so loud, stupid!"

"Okay. Okay. So anyway I'm turned off way before this. Like, I have on this super-duper skimpy lingerie and he got his socks on. But whatever, I'm in it now. So, I'm Rainbow Coalition-ing this thing, right." Joye throws her Fight the Power fist in the air. "Trying to keep hope alive, but it's not working. The sex was wack. Then, he passes out like he's tired. All I can think of is 'did he bore himself to death' because he can't possibly be asleep from that."

"Joye Allyn! If you don't shut the hell up!" Ro's phone rings, but she sends it to voicemail.

"I swear. I swear to God. I swear."

"So you were with him last night and you end up with Bryce for breakfast today?"

"Yes and no."

"Whatchu meeaaaann?! How? How Sway? How?"

"I mean, yes, I spent the night with Terry. But not last night, the night before last. I spent last night with Bryce." It was like Joye was conducting a symphony orchestra with all the hand motions she used to try to explain this mess she was in.

Mirroring her exaggerated hand movement, Ro continues to grill Joye, "But you left Terry's house yesterday morning?"

"Yessssss," Joye was embarrassed but Ro was her friend, and she was basically caught. She wouldn't lie to Ro anyway.

"You slept with Bryce too?"

"Yes, Lord, I did."

"I know you did, but humor me a little more than you already have, Crazy. You used protection with both right?"

"Yes, Mom, I did."

"That's kind of messed up, Joye. I mean, I don't want to judge you or anything but that's not even your style. What is going on with you? Like, seriously."

"You know, I don't know. I was so disappointed with Terry. Like, he had one job. Ya know? It's been so long since I had any, so I just really wanted to have a good time. But that's just not his area of expertise. And, when Bryce called, I swear to you, I tried to talk myself out of it. But I was just like why? If you're safe, you don't have to keep being deprived. So, not my best moment. But I don't feel bad about it."

"Oh no, I don't think you should feel bad. I'm just concerned. You know? You're typically the main one complaining about men using women and not being straight up or being safe with their bodies...so it just seems out of character."

"Oh, please! I'm not using anyone. They all got what they wanted too."

"So let's do this: Why do you think Terry went all out last night? Like, he pulled out all the stops. Did you sense that he wanted to maybe take it a step further with you?"

"He definitely made a grand gesture. But I don't know if I can get past the terrible sex. I can probably deal with the boring part but... I don't know. I just feel like if he would man the fuck up and take some initiative we could be happily in love, married, with four babies by now."

"Have you told him that?"

"Of course. I have told him that. What am I?"

"I'm just saying. Maybe he needs a little push or clarity from you." Ro realized that the waiter never called her name to grab her coffee and asked Joye to give her a second. When Ro got to the counter the cashier pointed out that her coffee was sitting at the pickup area. The coffee had gotten cold, so they promised to just bring her fresh cup to the table.

Ro came back to the table and picked the conversation up where she had left off. "Sorry. I was so indulged in your damn story I forgot to get my coffee. Now, what was I saying? Oh! I remember when y'all were dating and he broke up with you. You had a little attitude, but he said he had no idea that you would want to be in a serious relationship with him. So, I'm just saying, maybe he doesn't really know what you want."

"He knows. He just wants me to take the lead. I don't want to do that. But speaking of what someone wants: Bryce asked me to consider entering a committed relationship with him. Go fucking figure."

"Oh, you must have done some new tricks on his ass. Bryce ain't never talked about being serious with anybody or anything."

"Yeah, I did, but that's not why. He had a whole epiphany, and he said he's been thinking about it for a while and if he had to choose anyone to build a life with it would be me."

"That is unbelievable."

"I know. I was so shocked."

"I mean, I don't know him that well, but he's been sketchy since day one. Ya know? Always got women around and be dating everybody. I just don't believe he's ready."

"Ohhhh, you just like the boring guy because he's predictable and safe."

"And you just like the fun guy because he's unpredictable and a drama king. That excitement is going to wear off as soon as his ass cheats on you."

"Why would you say that? Bryce wouldn't even talk like this if he wasn't serious. Don't be putting that juju on my future husband with your Gayle King negativity."

"Oh my god. Future husband? You just got out of a relationship with your future husband! Speaking of losers, have you spoken to Elliott?"

"Nope. I am 100% sure that we are really done this time. I'm finally over him."

"Good. And, on that note, I have to get back to the 'burbs' babe." Ro grabbed her coffee. She had had more than enough of Joye's shenanigans, so she rolled her eyes and headed out of the cafe. She told Joye she'd chat with her later and made sure to mutter just loud enough for Joye to hear, "If you don't get your shit together..."

"Always focusing on the bad. Focus on the good, girl!"

"When are you going to grow up?"

"When I'm Neverty-nine! Deal with it." They both laughed and shook their heads.

Dr. Ellis lifted her head from her iPad when it sounded like Joye had put a period in her story. "How did your friend, Ro, make you feel when she shared her thoughts about what you told her?"

"Judged. I felt a little judged. But my friends always tell me the truth. I knew it was a bad decision, but I had made it. At that point, it didn't matter what anyone else thought about it. I own all of my mistakes and moved on with my day."

Joye sat in defense of a position that she wasn't one hundred percent in agreement with. She was thankful to have friends who loved her enough to tell her their truth about any and everything, but it didn't mean she wanted to hear it. Joye was still basking in the afterglow of being doted on these last couple of days. It didn't matter that she had hang-ups about each one of them; they both gave her something she wanted, and though she knew she didn't want anything more from them in return, she couldn't suppress the cuddle hormones that were causing her to fantasize about 'what-if'.

That was Joye; knowing exactly what she had but hoping to squeeze something more out of it. She wasn't like this with her friends and family or in her business, only with her men. It was as though she kept changing lovers to avoid changing herself. She would teeter along the precipice of being fully self-aware but then encumbering herself to situations that were much less than ideal in love. She was spending a good amount of her time shuttling between what she felt was familiar and safe under the ruling of her beliefs and ideas of what was accepted. Society told her that men didn't like women who had too many sex partners, so she recycled hers.

Problem solved. Right?

"No. I think I have admitted some of my wrongdoings as well. The biggest issue is me allowing it to go on for as long as it has." Joye barked at Dr. Ellis after the doctor made the observation that Joye spent a lot of time discussing what others do wrong, but didn't discuss how her actions may have contributed to the breakdown of her relationships.

"Do you know why you allow the relationships to go on for as long as they do?"

"Yes. If I love you, I love you. I think I should fight for us. I believe I should exhaust every option that I am capable of before throwing it away."

"Have you ever considered that you may not be aware of what the problem really is? Or that if you are aware that you may not be equipped with the proper knowledge, understanding, and tools to fix the issue at hand?"

"No. I haven't considered that. I figured it was just people finally realizing they didn't want the same things. Or maybe they were losing interest in each other."

"Good. It's perfectly normal to not know. I want to explore some of these ideas of what the problem truly is at a later session."

"Okay. Times up? Thanks, Doc."

Dr. Ellis winked at Joye and wished her well.

᠃

Girls' Night Out

Joye left Dr. Ellis' office and headed to meet Mallia, Kema, Jordin, and Ro. Mallia had an announcement to make, so she told the girls to meet her at The Optimist at 9 p.m. for drinks and dinner.

Joye thought she was running late, so she was rushing through the door. When she walked in she saw that Kema, Jordin, and Ro were already at the bar. "Hi, ladies!"

"Hey, girl." Ro, Kema, and Jordin responded.

Exchanging hugs and kisses Joye demanded, "Where's Mallia?" And, what the fuck does she have to announce? Do we have any idea?"

Making a confused face Jordin said, "I think it's an engagement y'all."

"What!? Are you serious? To who?" Joye let out. "What are y'all drinking?" Joye began to flag the bartender's attention.

Ro and Kema just shook their heads and shrugged their shoulders. They were as clueless as Joye.

Then Ro said, "I have a Wildflower."

"I just have Prosecco," said Kema. Jordin had not ordered a drink yet.

"May I have the Cain Cuvee Cabernet Blend please? Joye asked the bartender.

"She's texting me now." Jordin was responding to Mallia's text. "She's parking."

Jordin and Mallia were closer friends than the rest of the crew. It was no surprise that Jordin had the inside scoop about Mallia and no one else did.

"Whoa. I really can't believe she is engaged, and we don't know to who? That's crazy, right?" Joye was an open book among her friends so she expected to know what was going on in each of their lives as well. She sensed that something was off with Jordin's reluctance and secret body language, but she had no idea what the announcement might be.

"Me either, girl" Ro chimed in. "Maybe it's not an engage-ment. Maybe it's a promotion or something else important."

"Whatever it is. She needs to come on because I'm hungry." Kema said. "Ooh, there she goes."

Mallia was the absolute fitness guru between the five of them. She worked out every single day, so her body was sculpt-ed. She walked in seeming very nervous, but she was glowing and had a huge smile on her face. And because Jordin had al-ready let off that it may be an engagement everyone's eyes focused on Mallia's left hand.

The ladies begin making sounds and soft congratulatory screams, "Oh my god!" "What in the world!" "Who is this man?" "Girl, hurry up and tell us!" In the midst of the noise, the hostess came over to let them know that their table was ready and escorted them to their new seats.

"So?" Joye stared at Mallia. "What's the obvious news? Spill it!"

Mallia was very nervous. Kema, Ro, and Joye were looking at her and each other a bit concerned because there was such a silence about something that the girls would normally be bragging about.

Mallia took some deep breaths which made everyone even more tense. "Let me order my drink first."

"Aww, hell. This sounds like some bullshit." Leave it to Ro to call a thing a thing.

"Let her get her drink, Ro, before you start making judgments," Jordin said.

"Judgments? Girl, I'm just saying this doesn't seem like a happy announcement. If she has to get a drink before she even says anything then it's probably some bullshit." Ro was never one to bite her tongue, especially when annoyed.

The air in the room was not feeling like a fun girl's night.

The waiter brought Mallia's glass of wine. She took a sip and looked down at Joye. "I love you, Joye. You are my sister. You truly have been a wonderful friend to me."

Joye looked around and asked the table, "Am I getting dumped? What is happening?"

"Ah, shit." Ro threw her hands up in the air.

Joye responded calmly as she realized this wasn't a joke,

"Well, I love you too, Mallia. What's going on?"

"I wanted to share my good news with my girls, but I realize that it may not be good news for you."

"Why wouldn't it be good news for me, Mallia?"

Mallia held up her left hand to show off her sparkling sapphire engagement ring with a nervous smile. "Well, ladies, I am getting married!"

Everyone was looking at her waiting for the part that wasn't good news for Joye.

"To who? Who are you engaged to, Mallia?" Kema asked.

Mallia let out a huge sigh. "It's Abe."

There were cringing sighs, silence, the shaking of heads and "Ahh shits" covering the entire table. Everyone was disgusted with Mallia, except Jordin, who seemed to know what was going on all along.

"Abe as in Abraham Daniels? As in *my* Abraham Daniels? You're lying?" Joye giggled and dropped her head. This could not be true, but her gut was confirming that it was.

Mallia had tears in her eyes. "I'm not. I didn't mean to hurt you, Joye. I swear."

Joye was in complete and utter shock. How did this get by her? How did this even happen? Why would one of her best friends marry her ex?

Ro could not believe it. "Are you fucking serious? Like, how? Why would you—even... This is unreal."

Kema tried to make it all make sense. "So Mallia? You and Abe are a thing since when? And why did you keep this a secret up until now? You probably should have said something when you first fucked the dude."

"Wait. We haven't had sex. I have not fucked him." Mallia insisted. "Both of us have been abstaining from sex the whole time."

"Umm, what exactly is the whole time, Mallia?" Joye probed. "Yo, you are one shady bitch, Mal," Kema whispered.

"Joye I did not start talking to him until like nine months ago. I promise you."

"So nine months ago would be October/November of last year," Joye smirked and let out a little snicker. "Why wouldn't you tell me?"

"Everything just happened so unexpectedly, and I didn't know where it was going or if I really liked him or how to tell you? It just got out of hand and when he asked me to marry him yesterday, I knew I had to let you know. He's a great guy and I really am in love with him. I don't want to lose you. But I am in love with him, Joye."

"So he told you he hasn't had sex with anyone in nine months?" Joye stood up and began gathering her things.

"Yes. We both agreed to wait until we got married." Mallia explained.

Joye sighed and giggled again. "Well, congratulations. But do yourself a favor. Ask him where he stayed when he visited Atlanta in January and March. And then ask him how many times he had sex with that person. Don't start your life with this man with lies like he tried to do with me." Joye stormed out of the restaurant. She yelled back, "Somebody pay for my drink, please!"

"Ah, shit." Ro looked at Kema. "Can you cover her drink? Let me go get her."

She agreed, "Yes, I got it."

Ro looked at Mallia before she walked away from the table, "You ain't shit, Mallia. You know that right?"

Jordin moved into the seat next to Mallia and gave her a hug. "I know that was hard."

Kema interrupted Mallia and Jordin, "Hard? Hard my ass. It hasn't been hard for you to keep this secret from her for nine months! But now all of a sudden it's so hard for you." Kema mimicked the sounds of a damsel in distress. "And why would you do this shit in public? Do you know how embarrassing this is? " Kema brought her voice down, "You better be lucky she didn't turn this bitch into an episode of the housewives. Because, me? Oh, I would have dragged your ass all across this fucking restaurant."

"Take that ghetto mess up out of here, Kema," Jordin said as she signaled Kema away with a wave of her hand.

"Oh, I'm ghetto now? But your friend is about to husband community dick? Yeah, that's not ghetto at all. Both are y'all are dumb."

Jordin lashed back. "Oh, please, Kema! Joye has an assortment of niggas. Mallia just happened to fall in love with one of the many that's not good enough for her to keep around so she threw him away."

"You are missing the point you fucking dummy!" Kema lost it.

"Who are you calling a dummy?" Jordin was getting angry, but she knew not to cross Kema.

"You! This isn't about how many niggas she's had. This is about their friendship. But you don't see any betrayal in this scenario, do you? Fuck him! Okay. Nobody gives a shit about his Monkey-Paw Print having ass. And fuck you too for defending this bullshit."

Kema pointed at Mallia. "This muthafucka sat around all

of us all this time telling lies and denying a nigga and some dick? That's some ain't shit ass ghetto behavior if you ask me. Love don't hide. Only bullshit hides. Y'all some be best bitches. Ugh."

Kema walked out before her temper really blew a fuse. Jordin stayed back and consoled Mallia. Ro was in an Uber headed to Joye's place trying to keep her cool.

Kema: I almost had to fight these bitches!
Ro: WHAT?!
Ro: Meet us at Joye's place.
Kema: On my way!
Ro: She is upset but I couldn't get her to say anything the whole ride.
Kema: I'm gonna grab a bottle of whatever she was drinking here. I will be there in 15 minutes.
Ro: Cool

Kema turned around and walked over to the bar. "You do sell bottles to go, right?"

The bartender quickly answered, "Yes, we do! What can I get ya?"

"Great. Can I get the Cabernet Blend? I'm not sure which brand."

"No worries. We only have one. I got you covered."

"Thanks." Kema paid for the bottle and did her best to not look over at Jordin and Mallia but she couldn't help herself. When she did, she saw Abraham walking towards the table to meet them.

"This son of a bitch."

A familiar voice spoke to Kema, "Everything okay with your friend?" Kema turned around and saw one of her exes. "Kenny! Hey. What are you doing here?"

"It's one of my favorite spots," Kenny replied. "Is Joye good? I saw her run outta here."

"Oh, yeah. She's fine. Just a misunderstanding."

"Okay. Well, what have you been up to? I'd love to ca—."

"No. No, Kenny. We cannot catch up. We cannot exchange numbers. We cannot do anything, okay? Thanks for saying hello and checking on Joye. We're good though. Please take care of yourself." Kema left Kenny at the bar with the stupid face.

She mumbled to herself as she jumped in her car thinking about her friend and how messed up she must be. "What is this? Night of the living exes? Fuck."

Joye was sitting on her living room floor listening to Ro as she attempted to rationalize what Mallia had revealed at the restaurant. She wasn't accepting any of the excuses she heard as good enough.

"I don't know, Ro. She should have said something to me a long time ago."

"Yeah. She should have." There was a knock at the door. It was Kema. Ro leaped up to open the door; she could use the support in supporting Joye.

"Hey, babe. I have wine! How's she doing?" Ro signaled with her hands that she wasn't really sure of how Joye was doing. Kema immediately walked toward the kitchen to grab wine glasses and a bottle opener.

"Listen. Don't let this mess with you, babe. It's not worth it." Kema said as she began pouring wine for the ladies.

Joye was a bit numb and she was trying to answer a lot of questions in her head. She began speaking. "So they really thought this was okay? And, I-I am not saying that they are not in love. Hell, love does some strange things. But my best friend and ex? I mean, why wouldn't they just say 'Hey! This is what's happening! Don't want it to be any more awkward than it already is!' Don't surprise me with the news after it's a done deal.

"And you know what? I wouldn't have tried to talk her out of it. I wouldn't have hated on them. I would have said he's a great guy and he deserves love and maybe it's you that can give him that. I guess in the grand scheme of things my feelings about their lives together don't matter but..." Joye's voiced trailed off and she looked around the room like she was trying to find the right words. She couldn't remember if she had told the girls this piece of information, she was about to divulge but decided that she had no reason to lie or keep any secrets about her interaction with Abe post-breakup. "Y'all? He came to visit me twice this year! In January and in March. He spent two weekends with me. And we weren't abstaining from anything. He said when he was leaving my house, he was going to visit his friends. I had no idea that that included Mallia!"

"It's obvious that he is not that great of a guy, sis. He's lying to you. Lying to her. Using you for sex while he's here building a relationship with her. That's just trifling. That's not a great guy." Kema was hoping to remind Joye that this guy was not worth crying over.

Joye heard her but was still trying to reconcile what was going on. "Yeah. Maybe, but what is he trying to prove? Why go after my friend?"

Ro jumped in, "Why did she let him?"

"Now that's the better question. Skanky self." Kema agreed.

Joye did not like how she felt. She was certain that she didn't want Abe ever again, but she was uncertain about what she was feeling. She didn't know if she was upset that they both had lied to her by omission or that he had played her and her friend earlier in the year. She was unsure if she simply felt betrayed by him but mostly her friend. She was questioning her friendship, her relationship, her friend's behavior during her relationship, her intuition, and everything in between. She was wildly concerned at how she had been so picky when recognizing her tribe but still managed to choose too many of the wrong people to be in her life.

In searching for answers she was making excuses and accusations for every question she asked herself about this revelation.

"How do I even deserve this? What am I doing wrong? I tried to be a good girlfriend to him. I know I have been a good friend to her. I just don't understand." Joye expressed. Kema and Ro did not know what to say. All they wanted was to let her know that she didn't have to feel this pain alone. So they embraced her and sat with her until she was tucked into bed. They shoved vitamins down her throat and left fresh water on her nightstand. They told her they would check in on her first thing in the morning but not to hesitate to call either of them if she needed them before sunrise.

Joye was becoming fatigued with going through things that she felt she didn't deserve.

fami[LIAR] dick

Finding the [LIAR] in the Familiar

I talk about fear a lot.

It may not seem like it because I do a halfway decent job covering up my emotions when I want to appear tough. Fear disguised as pleasure is common in my world. Fear is the lie in place. Fear tells me that I'm not ready, so, in turn, I procrastinate. But the truth about procrastination is that I'm not ready to face the "ugly" truth, right?

So there are different types of truths for me: there's a "pretty" truth that makes me feel really good about myself. Then there's the "ugly" truth. The ugly truth makes me feel like crap. Sometimes the ugly truth makes me think I am a horrible person unworthy of love.

At the point when I decide whether to procrastinate or move forward with a man, I have already pondered the potential good outcomes versus the potential bad outcomes. It's the fear of hearing the potential bad outcome or "bad truth" as a response that slows me down when facing anything directly or head-on. The lie is that I probably have a really good grasp or sense of what the answer to the question is going to be.

Without studying, so many of us innately understand psychology, more than most of us would ever give ourselves credit for. So I understand that if I delay, delay, delay, more distractions will enter into my life, and the probability of me overlooking the real issue before me is high. But my fear of my truth says keep doing it this way.

I really need an answer now, but I'm afraid to hear it today.

I really want to resolve an issue, but I'm too fearful to face the ugly truth

I also know that it, whatever it is, will absolutely show its face later on in my life but hopefully, by that time, I'll have enough good things, good truths to cancel it out and move on. Sadly, this usually doesn't work out that way, and I found myself getting slapped in the face with constant reminders that "he ain't shit" and "y'all ain't never gonna be happy together except in bed."

Fear makes me lie to myself by convincing me that "I can just have sex with him this one time." And that it doesn't matter that I spent years in love with this man working very hard at trying to make a relationship work. I'm comfortable with him; he knows my body, and I don't have to add another number to my body count, which for the record, makes me not a whore.

It's true! I swear it is. What's funny about this thought process is when you use it as an analogy it sounds dumb as hell.

Check it out:

I had this couch that I really wanted to get rid of. It was old. It was ragged. It was filthy. Hell, it was even stinky at times. I hired professional cleaners ten times, and those nasty, ugly stains and dirty jeans smell just wouldn't come out. Every time the upholstery shop tried to repair it, it literally just kept falling apart. It was almost like it just wanted to be to'e up! But I must say, it was a very, very, very, very comfortable couch.

Anyway, trash day came along, and I told myself I was just gonna throw it out...finally! I was over it.

Seriously.

So, I took the couch to the dumpster because that's where it belonged. A few days went by, and I noticed one of my neighbors looking at the couch. This fool really wants my old, stinking ragged couch? Then I started thinking about all those clothes I was going to donate to Good-will but then my sister stopped by and tried on a bunch of those clothes and it looked really cute on her! So cute, that I got mad and told her that she was going through the wrong bag and that that stuff just needed to be dry cleaned, not donated.

That got my wheels rolling.

My neighbor was cute. She was pretty fly too. I wasn't about to let her have my old, ragged, stinking couch looking good in her place, so I decided that I was going to get my trash, I mean, my couch back. I moseyed on down to the dumpster and pulled the couch back into my house.

My daddy gave me that couch! That couch has sentimental value to me.

I miss that couch.

I spent six years of my life sitting on that couch.

That couch helped me through a lot of bad times.

That couch knows me, and I know it.

I'm comfortable with that couch.

I can keep it for a little while longer; it ain't gonna hurt nobody.

But yes, yes, it did and will continue to hurt someone. Me. But, back to my analogy.

I was sitting on a trash couch. Bacteria? Streptococcus? I don't know. It was literally trash, and I brought it back in the house because I was afraid that someone else would actually polish it up and make it better than I ever could. And I made the excuse that it was comfortable.

In reality, there are more comfortable couches in just about every furniture store on the planet. I decided I needed to get myself a new couch or maybe a gently used one and work with that one day.

No more trash couches.

chapter four

[CON]trol

Gaining

> *"There's a world out
> there that nobody has
> bothered to promise her."*
>
> - LAUREN DESTEFANO

Betray? Oh

Joye was familiar and maybe way too comfortable with losing a boyfriend because of betrayal. But this was the first time that she had come close to losing a good friend because of it. Joye's perspective was that this didn't have to be an end to a long term friendship. She valued and respected love enough to know that it doesn't always show up in a way that makes sense. Love was love. And there is no written law that said her friend and her ex couldn't happen upon love and happiness together. Had Joye been given the proper warning, she was sure she could have handled the awkward situation she now found herself in. Even though she was still furious with

Mallia, Joye hadn't drawn a hard line about the friendship. Actually, she was sure she could move beyond it. But when?

Joye skipped her morning jog that day; she had to make calls and work on an end of the day proposal deadline. She had shit to do, so sitting and dealing with the BS would have to wait.

Joye opened her brand new Keurig and tried out the four African coffee pods: two Ethiopian, one Congo, and one Tanzanian. Her dirty mind immediately selected Congo because she'd read that Congo men had the biggest dicks on the planet, and Joye liked her coffee like she liked her dicks: big, black and sweet.

Once her coffee was brewed, she positioned herself on her couch for several hours. Handling her business was one of her pride and joys in life. She always seemed to go harder and be more productive when things were out of order with her emotionally. It was like her indifference to her feelings was fuel to her work flame. She was trying to avoid what was on her mind and in her heart, but she failed because she kept being distracted by her thoughts, and by Kema and Ro.

Ever since the big announcement, Kema and Ro had been calling and texting non-stop. Even though Joye returned their texts, she was busy with clients and potential clients, so she couldn't call them.

As soon as Joye pressed send on the last client email, she closed her laptop and called Ro.

"Ro?"

"Hey, girl! Sorry to blow up your phone like that. I was just making sure you were good."

"I'm good. Just working, that's all."

"Okay. I'll call you later." Ro hung up.

Before she could finish telling Siri to call Kema, Kema called again. Joye answered the phone singing Kema's name to the opening of "Buddy" by De La Soul. *"Kema, Kema, Kema, Kema!"*

Kema knew immediately what was happening when Joye answered the call and jumped right into the song, *"Say what?"*

They both sang the first verse of the hip-hop classic together.

Kema laughed. "Ayeeeee! You sound like you're feeling better."

"I'm good, girl. Just working. You know?" She lied.

"You sure?"

"Yeah. We still good for this Saturday, right?"

"Yup. I'll talk to you before then."

"Cool. Later. I gotta get back to work." But that was also a lie. She was done with her work. She just wanted to get off the phone and loaf around for the rest of the night.

She grabbed snacks from the kitchen, refilled her coffee cup, and repositioned her butt back on the couch with her face buried in her phone.

She browsed Instagram and Facebook liking posts and reading comments. The day turned into an entire afternoon and early evening in conversation and text. Monkey Paw Prints texted. She left him on read.

Abe: Hey. Can you talk?
Joye: 'Read'
Abe: I want to explain if you will allow me to.
Joye: 'Read'
Abe: If not I understand.
Joye: 'Read'

Joye didn't want to engage prematurely with Abe, Mallia, or Jordin. She wanted to be thoughtful and free from reacting to her emotions. These were all people that she had loved or shared some type of bond with. While her feelings were hurt, she was serious about her relationships and didn't throw people away easily.

She also wanted to talk to Dr. Ellis about it. She had heard from Abe pretty quickly since the news broke last night, but she hadn't heard a peep from her girls, Mallia and Jordin. She wasn't feeling that at all. Even though it was hard for her not to respond to Abe and tell him to kick hot rocks barefoot, she put him on ice and muted all text notifications from him. Her mom had called earlier, so she called her back.

"Hey, Ma. What you doing?"

"Heyyy. I just finished exercising. About to get in the shower."

Joye thought about how beautiful her mom already was. Mrs. Cynthia Allyn was simplistically gorgeous. She had full lips and high cheekbones. Her caramel skin was flawless, her gray hair was natural, fluffy, and healthy-looking. She didn't wear makeup unless she was going out. She dressed casually and comfortably unless she had an event to attend. She was tall, 5'9", so no matter what she wore it looked classy and like it came straight off the runway. Mrs. Allyn had that quintessential 1970s black beauty, and she never let that part of herself go.

After her husband had passed, Cynthia had time to focus on herself. For 45 years, she was a caretaker: first to her two children, and then later to her husband. But now life was different, and she was slowly but surely finding a new routine. Joye was excited to see her mom focusing on her physical fitness.

"Okay sexy thick."

"What!?" Her mother was cool, but not that cool.

"Nothing. I missed your call last night. I was out with the ladies. So I'm just calling you back."

"How's everybody?"

"Crazy. I gotta tell you about Mallia when I see you."

"What did she do now?"

"You said that like she's always getting into something."

"From where I sit, she's always been slick. So whatever it is I'm sure I won't be surprised."

"Uh uh! Well, we may not be friends anymore after this, but we'll see."

"That's fine. People grow up and out of people all the time. It's just a part of life. Plus, it's time out for idiots anyway. You can love people but over there." Cynthia said as she pointed off into the distance. She didn't care if Joye and Mallia never spoke again because she never liked Mallia in the first place.

"Oop! Now Mrs. Allyn? You better preach that word! Anyway, Ma. Mel and I wanna come visit in a few months. I'll let you know the exact dates. We're staying with you too."

"Oh, good. Y'all bringing my grandbaby?"

"Nope! Melanie said Sara has to stay with her pappy. I think she needs a break."

"Well, I'll be here. I'll get the rooms cleared out."

"Uh uh. We're sleeping in the bed with you, homegirl!"

"Not happening. Y'all talk too much."

"Dang, Ma! Alright, let me get back to it. I'll call you later. Love you."

"Love you too, baby. Oh! I have something important to tell you girls when you get here. Don't let me forget."

"What's so important that you can't remember to remember? Why is that my job?" Joye crinkled up her entire face in irritation of her mom's request.

"I'm serious. Just remind me. Now I have to go," she said, and abruptly hung up the phone.

Joye was vexed that her mom had given her a job and didn't allow her to ask any qualifying questions before jumping off of the phone. She started talking to herself. "Why I gotta remember? Shit." Joye was complaining at the same time that she was putting an appointment on her calendar to remind her mother to tell her something important. While she was doing that, Bryce texted.

> **Bryce:** Wyd
>
> **Joye:** Nothing. Wyd?
>
> **Bryce:** Waiting for you
>
> **Joye:** Umm, Sir. You can't be serious. Waiting for me to what?
>
> **Bryce:** Be my woman.
>
> **Joye:** Ha!
>
> **Bryce:** It's like that? Damn.
>
> **Joye:** No. Just kidding. Come over. I've thought about it. We should talk.
>
> **Bryce:** That doesn't sound good. Maybe I should just call.
>
> **Joye:** Oh, it's good. Just come over.
>
> **Bryce:** See you in an hour.

When Bryce asked Joye to consider entering a serious relationship with him, she did just that. That night was the beginning of them working to sort out the details of their committed relationship. There was some history between them, so it wasn't a difficult transition for them. Plus, Joye wanted to be in a real relationship. It had only been a few days since Bryce had asked her to think about their relationship. She hadn't heard a peep from Terry since she last saw him and Jamel hadn't contacted her either. She had also just found out that her ex was going to marry her best friend. With everything that was going on, Joye thought entertaining Bryce's proposition was the next best move for her.

෪

The Wait for Love

Things were moving really fast since Joye and Bryce had their committed relationship talk. They had found a nice routine that they were satisfied with. They enjoyed spending time together and they made a pact that once a month they'd have a "real" date. Bryce had the honor of planning the first monthly date. He arrived at Joye's house a little early. He thought he was giving her ample time to get dressed for their date night. Instead the energy between them was off. Joye interpreted Bryce's demeanor as frustrated and standoffish so she began complaining and an argument ensued.

"I want you to love and consider me the way I have loved and been considerate of you." Joye stormed out of her bathroom to look Bryce directly in his eyes as she made her demand. "Is that really too much to ask for?"

She felt like she was talking to a child, but he was an adult man with two Masters' degrees.

"I don't know how to do that," Bryce said while thinking about why he avoided relationships for so long.

"I have been telling you exactly how to do it. You just don't listen." Joye had been walking back and forth between her bedroom where Bryce was standing, her bathroom where she was attempting to brush her teeth, and her closet because she kept making different clothing selections.

Bryce slowly walked over to take a seat on the bench at the end of the bed. He leaned over and placed his head in his hands. "Here you go playing victim again."

"How did I become the last thing of importance in your life?"

"Baby, you're not unimportant. You're impossible!"

"Impossible? What does that even mean?"

"Joye, baby. You don't have to be this damn strong. All it says to me is that you don't need me."

"Oh my god. Yes. Yes, I am strong. Not because I don't need you though, but because you don't show up for me when I *do* need you. Have you ever considered that?" Joye said after finally deciding on what to wear and placing her dress on the bed. "That sometimes the issues I may have are to be addressed in the moment they are presented to you and not at your convenience?" Joye continued. "When everything else on your list of things to do is checked off. Maybe you forfeit the opportunity to feel needed because you just don't have time for me." Joye kept talking as she walked back into her closet to grab a pair of shoes. "You're so busy running off being everybody's goddamn hero all the time." When Joye walked back into the bedroom she took a seat next to Bryce and began trying on the shoes she picked out. She turned to Bryce and asked, "But what about me? Hell, what about you?! You are not making time to take care of yourself. Don't you think that's important?"

Bryce had heard this before from Joye. She would tell him that he left her hanging and she felt alone in their relationship way more than what felt appropriate. Tonight, it struck a chord with him. "Baby, I'm trying. I really am."

"Really? So why isn't it working?" She was snarky when she shouldn't be. Bryce reached out to touch her hand, but she swiftly got up and walked away from him. Bryce needed her to hear that he was trying, but all Joye heard was him acknowledging that he was failing.

Bryce was insulted. "Why isn't it working?" He stood up and walked over to her and got in her face. "It's not working because of you!"

Joye brushed him off and immediately turned away from him to walk into the bathroom and adjust her makeup as Bryce continued, "Do you hear yourself?" he mimicked Joye. "'Why isn't it working?' You want instant results. I have a hundred thousand things on my plate. You don't think I'm concerned about my health? About you?"

"I don't. And I don't think I should have to beg you. I am sick and tired of asking you to take care of yourself."

Bryce was indeed worried about his health. He also was worried that Joye wasn't happy with him. He thought working to make their lives comfortable in other ways was even more important. In the event that his health took a turn for the worst, he could have the care he needed, and she would be okay.

Tonight was supposed to be a fun and special night for them, but instead of getting out of the house for a good time and giving Joye what he thought she wanted, she started an argument because he had missed his last two doctor's appointments but was making her get dressed up for what he described to her as a 'work function' at the last minute.

He wrapped his arms around Joye's waist from behind. She pretended that the closeness didn't affect her and continued to put her earrings on. They gazed at each other's reflections in the mirror.

Another beautiful *looking* couple.

"I'm terrified," Joye said softly to Bryce as she lowered her eyes. That was a loaded confession. She was embarrassed by how she verbalized her fear about his health. From her unauthorized and non-clinical eyes, his health was declining and he seemed to not care. She could only think about the quality of life they would have.

Would he die?

Would he get too sick and require around the clock care?

How would they afford him being so sick so young?

Would she have to give up her dreams to become a caretaker?

"I'm terrified" also summed up how she felt about moving forward in this relationship with him. She was unsure, and her intuition was telling her this was not a good idea. She was having an internal battle with herself about seeing this relationship through despite her reservations or ending it

"Baby, I know. I am too. I promise I will not miss another appointment. I'm going to be okay. Stop worrying so much. You hear me?" She nodded yes. He kissed her on the cheek. Then he humped her ass like a dog and barked. They both laughed.

"Let's get out of here before we miss your thing."

Bryce yelled out, "Woof!"

"Oh, God, please don't rip your shirt off tonight. This is work. Don't scare those people." Nobody took their fraternity more seriously than an Omega Man.

§

The ride to Bryce's work event was short but felt like forever. Bryce did the majority of the talking. He reminisced about his college days at Florida A & M University (FAMU). He told stories about his fraternity brothers and how so many of them had come so far in life and in their careers. He talked about being the only male in his friend group who was unmarried without children. He went on and on about everything. They laughed. They laughed a lot during that ride.

When Bryce pulled into the parking lot to park the car, Joye recognized where they were. It was the Foundry at Puritan Mill, one of her favorite venues in the city.

"Ooh, y'all fancy. I love this place."

Bryce just smiled at her. They walked hand in hand up the sidewalk and to the front door where they were greeted by a doorman. Joye thought *A doorman? This is new.* She asked Bryce, "What do y'all have going on in here? A dinner or something?"

But when they walked in, Joye saw some of her friends, her sister and brother-in-law, Bryce's mother, and all of his friends. They cheered and shouted with every step she and Bryce took towards them.

Her heart dropped.

She knew what this was.

She turned to Bryce who had a huge smile on his face and was squeezing her hand tightly, partially from excitement and partially from nervousness, but it was too late. Her eyes were filled with tears that were far from happy. In her mind she was thinking, *Please, do not do this*, or *Get me the fuck out of here*! She could not believe this was about to happen. She turned to him and buried her face into his chest. The crowd let out a loud "Aww" but that was not in order with what she was feeling.

She was upset.

Bryce was either too nervous to see, too in the moment to care, or in too deep having made a big deal and invited all of their loved ones that he had to follow through.

He managed to lift her head and turn to the crowd to say a few words.

"Umm, thank you guys for helping to make tonight a special night for me and Joye. Some of you traveled far to be here and I appreciate it. To my mom, it means a lot to have you in the room with us." He cleared his throat and one of his boys called out from the crowd, "You got this FreaQUE-B!" and all of his frat brothers began barking.

"Man. Cut it out! Cut it out. No, seriously. Joye is an amazing—amazing woman. I tell people all the time how she made me want to change my whole life and just be a better man. So here we are." Bryce was nervously rubbing his hands together and swaying back and forth a bit as he continued to talk.

Joye didn't hear a word he said. Everything that came out of his mouth sounded like the teacher from Charlie Brown. She stood there with a smile on her face and her eyebrows raised. She was looking over the crowd. Her sister, Melanie and Kyle, were grinning from ear to ear. Kema was smiling, Ro had the *I-know-you-fucking-lying* look on her face. They recognized how horrified Joye looked. Jordin and Mallia were there whispering back and forth in their own conversation. Joye got pissed off for another reason after seeing them there. They were also wondering where Joye's mother wasn't there. Joye was thinking the same thing. This could not go down like this.

Bryce pulled the ring box from the inside pocket on his jacket and grabbed Joye's left hand. "Joye Allyn, you are the most beautiful and most amazing woman I have ever known. I want to spend the rest of my life with you, so I'm asking you in front of all these people. Will you marry me?"

Joye could not embarrass this man. She would never embarrass this man in public. She smiled gently, nodded her head up and down rapidly, and said ever so gently, "Yes."

Bryce wanted to hear her. "Is that a yes? Let me hear it." He encouraged her to get louder.

"Yes." Joye belted out to not cause a scene.

Bryce slid the almost 2-carat, pear-shaped diamond ring onto her finger. He stood up and kissed Joye. He was excited. He shouted to the audience, "Ya boy's engaged!"

He was slapping hands, hugging people, and moving all over the room. Joye was stuck in the same place he left her as people gathered to congratulate and celebrate with her. Joye didn't know what to do with herself.

The music began to play, and food started to be rolled out. It was an engagement party with lots of side-eyes, doubt, and a future bride who was not ready to marry the future groom.

Their engagement lasted only 26 days.

She told Bryce during their car ride home that she couldn't believe he proposed. She also explained that she wasn't ready to be married to him. He told her that she was just nervous and intimidated at the thought of merging lives and asked her to "sleep on it." She complied, and they tabled the conversation for the next day.

The next day came, but the conversation didn't. Joye tried to get Bryce to sit down and talk as planned, but he was so busy he kept postponing.

Their mornings were fast-paced. Their evenings were exhausted. He had been coming over every night to spend it with her, but it was consistently after midnight. She would try to stay awake for his arrival, but she'd often fall asleep. When she was awake, he was too tired to talk, and since she didn't want to be that chick who didn't let her man sleep, she let him be.

Ten days passed.

They had not shared two sentences about their engagement.

They didn't even have sex.

Nineteen days passed.

Joye was aggravated. She tried everything to get Bryce to talk about their engagement, but no luck. Plus, he was not giving up the D *and* he was rejecting her advances.

That was unlike him in all the years she had known him. She worried that his health was interfering with his sex drive.

Joye: Babe, I know you've been working late. But you being tired so much has me worried. Are you feeling ok? Have you been to the doctor?

Bryce: I'm fine. Not yet.

Joye: Do you want me to see if I can get you another appointment sooner?

Bryce: No.

Joye: Ok. I'll see you tonight.

Twenty days passed.

She asked nicely. She reminded him daily. She sent text messages inquiring if "tonight was okay?" She was doing her best to remain calm and sweet but, again, she found herself feeling ignored, dismissed, and unimportant. She asked herself a hundred times over the course of those twenty days, *What could be more important than discussing our engagement?* Joye's patience ran out.

She was already on the fence about the relationship and she was getting really tired of pretending to be okay with how Bryce was handling things. She believed that his cold-shouldering this conversation was not only a clear sign of his avoidance issues but also that something was severely wrong with the relationship.

On the 26th day, she was totally on edge. She wasn't sure if she was just being insecure or if there was more to what was happening between her and Bryce. She called Kema to vent, hoping she would help settle her fears.

Kema was at home doing squats when Joye called. She turned her music down so she could really focus on what Joye was telling her. "And, he's not saying *anything*?"

"Not really. He just keeps blowing me off and I'm starting to get that feeling in my gut."

"I mean, Joye, he took this long to decide to get married. Surely he got rid of his hoes."

"It just doesn't add up. I mean, maybe he's just really angry about me saying I was nervous about the marriage."

"Who's not nervous about getting married? It's a big deal."

"Well, maybe it made him more nervous? I don't know. But it doesn't feel like it's as simple as nerves. The man is literally not talking to me. Like this is our engagement period. We should definitely be talking and having lots of sex."

"Wait. No sex? Girl, goodbye."

"Barely. But maybe he's just not feeling well. Ya know?"

"Then he needs to tell you that, Joye. Stop making excuses for him."

"I'm not! I'm trying to figure this out without being a bitch."

"Yeah, but he might need to get cussed out. This is ridiculous. Are y'all eating together? Playing games? Watching TV? Anything?"

"No. He leaves early and comes back really late. That's been the dance since the night after the engagement."

"At your house?"

"Yeah."

"So, you haven't been to his house in three wee—almost a month?"

"No."

"Why not?" Kema paused for a moment knowing Joye didn't have answers. "Maybe he's stressed about not being at his own house? Okay, just go to his house tonight and spend some time over there. He may just need to be in his own element."

Joye hadn't given the living arrangements idea much thought. He hadn't slept in his bed in a while, and though no one forced him to make this decision, she agreed that could be a contributing factor to whatever was happening with them.

"That's why they pay you the big bucks, Ke! I'm gonna send this email and then head over there. Thanks, boo!"

Joye felt a little better after talking to Kema. She thought she had tried everything, but this was one thing she had not considered. Later in the day, ignoring her nasty gut feeling,

Joye decided to reroute the evening for her and Bryce. She gathered a few things from her place, ran a few errands to make sure they had snacks, and picked up dinner from Busy Bee Cafe, his favorite soul food restaurant.

About 7 o'clock that night she texted Bryce and asked what time he thought he'd be home. He told her around or after midnight: the usual. She was literally one block away from his house when she responded.

Joye: Dinner at your house tonight. I'll be there in 5 minutes. Meet you there for a late night rendezvous.

Her phone rang immediately.

She was happy to get a call from him. He hadn't done that in a while.

"Hi, Baby!"

"What do you mean you'll be at my house in 5?"

"Well hello to you, too." Bryce was talking over her and almost screaming. "I was just thinking it would be nice to spend time at your place. Sleep in your bed? Make it easier for you to get your day started?"

But Bryce did not agree. "Just go home man. We can do that at your place."

"What? Why are you going off? I'm already here." Joye's chest began to heat up as she made the final turn onto his street. There was no logical reason for him to not want to be at his house. That filthy gut feeling kicked in again.

She turned into his driveway and pressed the garage door button. There were two cars parked: his and another she had never seen before.

"What the fuck?" She parked, closed her eyes, and took a deep breath. She knew what was about to happen.

Bryce opened the entry door from the garage and began walking out. He had on his basketball shorts and a t-shirt. Joye thought *that's a comfortable look for someone who is supposed to be at work*. Joye walked through the garage without saying a word trying to make her way to the door to enter the house, but he kept blocking her.

"Babe? Babe? Babe!" Bryce kept repeating as he tried to grab her. But Joye kept dodging him and asking questions. "What are you doing? Why are you here? So, I can't go in your house now?"

"Babe? Listen. Listen. Listen." Bryce didn't really know what to do and he definitely didn't know what to say.

"Whose car is that?"

A beautiful woman appeared at the door with a confused and frightened look on her face. She was very tall, athletic, with long dark hair. She wore oversized glasses and had on yellow track shorts and a tie-dyed t-shirt. She had a yellow plastic cleaning glove on one hand and a spray bottle in the other. For a hot second, Joye thought she could be the cleaning lady. But then reality slapped her right in the face.

"That's my rental car." The woman responded to Joye. Then she turned to Bryce, "Babe? What's going on?"

"You have got to be shitting me," Joye said a little under her breath but loud enough for everyone to hear. She looked at Bryce with a look of complete disbelief but no anger. She was partially relieved.

Bryce tried to summon words from his mouth, but he struggled. He dropped his head and put his hands in his pockets. Joye pushed him out of the way and reached out to shake the woman's hand.

"Hi, I'm Joye, his fiancé."

"Fiancé! Bryce? What is she talking about? I know you didn't pull me into a mess like this."

Joye stepped in the door and walked to the kitchen. She waved for everyone to follow her. "Let's huddle, team," she said sarcastically.

Joye opened a cabinet and grabbed a 400 dollar bottle of Glenlivet 25-Year-Old XXV scotch, and poured them all a glass, neat. She intended to be mature as she addressed what was unfolding before her eyes, but she fell short. She took a sip of her drink then she started talking.

This," pointing to Bryce, "nigga proposed to me 26 days ago." Then she turned to the woman, "Yep. Twenty-six days. Umm, wha-what is your name?"

The woman quickly responded, "Sierra."

"Sierra. Okay, I don't know how long you and Bryce have been fucking, but," turning toward Bryce again, "He's been distant and only coming home to sleep, and now I know why."

Joye went on to lay it all out on the table for the two strangers in the room with her. She wasn't trying to hurt the lady. She just wanted to get some shit off of her chest. As for Bryce, she didn't have any considerations for him during the conversation.

Sierra took a seat on one of the barstools in the kitchen. Joye kept venting and drinking.

"You know, you would think a man who proposed to a woman just a few weeks ago would actually be beyond this kind of bullshit, huh?" Joye could feel her emotions rising. She didn't want to get upset, so she redirected her rant towards Bryce. "I guess you never can really know a nigga. Speaking of not knowing a nigga, Bryce...so we're fucking strangers and letting them stay in our houses now? Is that what we're doing, *fiancé*?"

Bryce was uncomfortable and literally unable to get any words outside of "I" to form. His mouth was opening, and he was stammering with his heavy sighs.

Sierra jumped into the conversation hoping to clear her name. "I have to apologize to you. I'm honestly just as shocked as you are. Bryce never mentioned that he had a girlfriend let alone a fiancé."

There was a moment of silence. Joye stared at Sierra.

"I hope you're not expecting me to accept that apology?" Bryce was stressed out, rubbing his jaw and contemplating his next move.

"Not at all. I just want you to know the truth." Sierra went on to share her story of meeting Bryce in person two nights before their engagement at a lunch convention. They had been working together on a virtual project and had gotten pretty chum chummy over the phone and Skype meetings.

"In all the times we talked he insisted that he was," Sierra made air quotes, "Very single" every time I asked him if he was in a relationship," Sierra explained that she lived out of town and she and Bryce had an instant and very sexual connection once meeting face-to-face then he offered up his place. "I had no reason to believe I was in the middle of some mess," she insisted.

Joye was really annoyed that Bryce had nothing to say. "Bryce? Is this true?" Bryce just scratched his head and looked away in shame.

Sierra jumped in again, "I'm telling you the truth. I've been here for a couple of weeks now. We've been working non-stop--"

"So fucking him is part of your job? That's work?"

"I'll take that. I just want you to know that under normal circumstances, yes, I would have been concerned about his behavior. The coming and going. But Bryce told me he had an older sister that was sick. He said he had to spend the nights with her because she did not have an overnight caretaker. I just felt like I didn't have the right to ask more questions."

Joye was shocked. Joye took the last sip of her drink, glanced at Bryce, snickered, and said, "That's an elaborate lie, nigga."

Bryce was sitting at his dining table with his head down.

Joye was done talking and listening. She put her keys to his house on his kitchen counter, then went to her car to get the garage door opener, and sat it next to her keys. She slowly walked over to Bryce, making sure he saw her sliding the ring from her finger. She paused when she got the ring to the tip of her finger. Then she took his hand, put the ring in it, grabbed his face, and held it for a moment.

"Take care of yourself, okay?" she said, then kissed him on both cheeks.

And then she left.

୫

That night, she felt nothing. Unsure if she was just numb or some kind of savage beast she chose to not harp on it. She took a hot shower, put her bonnet on, and slipped into her comfy pajamas and fluffy socks. She heated up the soul food she had bought earlier and posted up in her bed with the remote control. She wasn't thinking about Bryce or worried about what her friends and family might say. She was literally trying to find something good to watch. Between Hulu, Prime Video, and Netflix there were way too many choices. So she settled on reruns of *Law & Order: Special Victims Unit*. You can never go wrong with that.

Halfway into dinner and binging on Detective Benson and Stabler's bullshit she heard keys jangling to open her front door. The alarm beeped a few times, and she could hear the code being entered. That could only be one person: Bryce. She didn't grab her keys from him when left.

Joye didn't budge.

She stayed in bed watching television and chomping down on fried chicken and collard greens. She didn't normally eat like that, so this was a treat for her and the enthusiasm in her chewing was proof.

Bryce dragged his bad body language into her bedroom.

"Can we talk?"

Joye ignored him. It was like he wasn't there. Bryce asked again, "Joye? Can we talk?" Crickets.

Bryce walked over to Joye's bed, picked up the remote, and powered the TV off. "I said, can we talk?"

Joye licked her fingers and looked around the bed for the paper towels she brought for the greasy mess she intended to make. She wiped her hands, sat up tall, and crossed her legs Indian-style. She looked at him with the *Oh-so-now-you-wanna-talk-nigga* facial expression.

Bryce took a deep breath. "Joye. It was never my intention to hurt you. I really thought I was ready to take us to another level. I am sorry. I am sorry for embarrassing you. I am sorry for everything."

He paused a few times hoping Joye would respond, but she didn't. She just continued to listen and stare.

Bryce took in another deep breath. "I-uh. I-I know you probably don't care about my side of what went down or why but I want to tell you that I-I freaked out—"

Joye barked and yelled, "FreaQUE-B!" It was totally her intention to be an asshole.

"I deserve that. Are you okay?"

"I'm fine."

"Really?" Joye nodded yes. "So, you really didn't want to get married to me?"

"*I* wanted to try. I just—*I* got nervous. But *you*? *You* got distant and *you* got a girlfriend. Literally two days after your proposal. What a joke. *You* needed a three-week vacation, and we weren't even 48 hours into our engagement. But *you*, you're over here asking *me* if *I* wanted to get married. The fucking nerve."

"I know. I know. I'm not even going to try to explain that fuck shit but you're right. I wasn't ready. All I can say is, I can get this right. I know I can. If you let me. I will get this right."

"Let's just be honest with each other. I'm not ready. You're not ready. It's simple. No hurt. No games. Just move on with our lives."

Bryce could not wrap his mind around failing at this relationship. He had purposely waited until he was certain that he wanted a new type of life before asking Joye to take this step with him. Even though he had messed up royally, as Joye's mom would say, he couldn't understand how Joye could give up on him. He wanted her to fight for him. He needed her to fight for him.

But she knew that it was time for her to take care of herself and give up these pseudo-relationships that exploited her need for validation and intimacy. A 26-day engagement was quite the wake-up call.

"That was our last chance. I want to do better. I have to do better. I need to get my shit together."

Bryce accepted that there was no changing her mind. Joye got out of her bed and walked toward him. He nodded acknowledging his defeat. "Joye?"

Joye put her hand out and demanded, "My key."

❦

A week later, Joye finalized her and Melanie's trip home to see their mom. She switched her in-person counseling session with Dr. Ellis to a telehealth session and needed to prepare for that call.

During this session, she went in-depth about why she accepted a marriage proposal to protect her man from public humiliation. Dr. Ellis was able to bring her to accept responsibility for entering a relationship because she wanted to clean up and cover up her unacceptable sexual encounters. Joye was disappointed in herself.

"So, you believe I chose to be in that relationship as a correction for sleeping with two men back-to-back?" Joye questioned.

"Is that the reason?" Dr. Ellis sent the tennis ball back over the net.

"Man. Maybe so? I've never thought of it like that." Joye sat up on her couch and looked up toward the ceiling as if she could see her thoughts moving around. "I thought I was just being open, trying something new, or giving him a chance, but maybe it was just a big ol' conniving justification to myself. Hmm?"

Dr. Ellis chimed in, "I can't tell you the reason. But as you think through these things and allow yourself to be honest with yourself, you'll be able to distinguish fact from fantasy."

Joye nodded in agreement. "You know what else I wanted to mention, Dr. Ellis? My ex and one of my closest friends are engaged now?"

"Are you surprised or angry? How do you feel about it?"

"I don't know. I think I feel betrayed. I mean, I actually had sex with him while they were apparently dating, and I had no idea that they were even a thing. So, I guess, first I feel bad?"

"You feel bad about sleeping with your friend's boyfriend?"

"Yeah, I guess. Now that I know they were seeing each other. But I also feel bad for her because he was lying to both of us at that time. Like, why would you want to marry a guy like that? I can get over him being my ex-boyfriend part, but not the liar and a cheater part. Like he knowingly put us both in a bad way. If I had known—if someone had just told me I could have prevented all that. I mean, I'm not upset that they are together, but I think they could have told me. That blows my mind."

"Joye you are not responsible for either of them, and you can't control their behavior. I see how you being caught up in their relationship without having all the facts can bother you."

"Yeah. I gotta sleep on that one, Doc. I just don't understand that."

"Well, you don't have to understand everything that happens. Sometimes it's simply about accepting what is and moving on."

Dr. Ellis was absolutely right. But Joye would spend days and nights trying to crack codes and figure things out. She was a bottom-line person. Everything had to make sense and she demanded details to get to an understanding. Joye acknowledged that accepting things as they were was one of her greatest challenges, but she was working hard to change that train of thought. Joye decided that it was more important for her to be happy than to be right.

"Good talk, Dr. Ellis. Thank you. I'll schedule my next appointment through your portal. Goodnight."

Joye felt like she was getting a hold of herself. She picked up her journal and began jotting down more and more of her truths.

It was time for her to close the chapter on a lot of things in her life and begin writing a few new ones.

gaining [CON]trol

Finding the [CON] in Control

As I journal, I am able to go back and analyze my story. It becomes clear what my patterns are. Through my relationships, I have been very forceful in trying to obtain what it is I felt I needed. In that forcefulness, whether it be language, tone, or anything else that would appear as aggression, I was never really well received by my partner(s). I definitely wasn't received in the way that I intended or expected to be, that's for sure. No one can hear me, the same as I can't hear anyone when they are at this frequency.

I started to recognize the slight and subtle differences in the delivery of how I spoke to people, in particular, how I spoke to the men I dated. Early on in the journal, I noticed that I was stern, sarcastic, and witty. I'm not as harsh in the way I spoke to Monkey-Paw Prints as I was with Scrabble Man. I have been an extremely aggressive, foul mouth, determined woman who wants to force my issues and make my partners give me what I want because, fuck this shit; I deserve it.

Through journaling I've created a safe and sacred space for me to reflect and develop a discovery process to help me learn more about not only who I am but why I am and what all of my intimate interactions and experiences, even those not mentioned in this entry, says about me. While I know deep down that I deserve all these things that I'm fighting for, there's still so much work to be done to show people that they can give these to me or that I am even ready to receive all of it. Honestly, that's been one of the most difficult things for me to accept about who I am and how I behave in my life.

I don't know where this notion that I'm supposed to fight for everything I deserve came from other than just being without in so many areas of my life. Today, this is simply not good enough. I can't lean on that excuse anymore. I think the re-messaging has to be to live my life in a way and behave in a way that matches the things that I know I deserve if I really want to receive them. Not to mention, you teach people how to treat you so it is now apparent that my demands did not always match my behavior because if it did more people would have been willing to give those things to me. There would be no need for me to put up such a fight. That in and of itself is quite powerful for me as I move into this next phase of whatever my life is. Of course, there are some ain't shit ass people in this world that will attempt to treat me like nothing because of who they are, but my acceptance of their treatment is a direct and immediate reflection of who I am.

The lack of control of myself caused me to invite men into my life who lacked control of themselves. Their lack of control translated into many different types of behaviors from irresponsibility to infidelity, from verbal abuse to financial abuse, from being inconsistent and unavailable to displaying signs of alcoholism and other dependent and code-pendent attributes.

Excluding the teenage and adult men who violated my trust when I was a minor — I don't, and neither should any person on this side of that card — take the blame for the indecency of others. Those negative attributes — or vices — are clear demonstrations of their lack of control of themselves. But as an adult, because I had already lost control myself, I allowed this bad behavior in and around my life from everyone and in every relationship.

That's the line, the common line that I can draw through all of my relationships: losing control, lack of control, being forceful and demanding, and at the top of the list, the desire and need to be made first. The desire and need to be someone else's priority.

I made all of my guys, at some point in the relationship, my priority, not because they were always worthy but because it's the prototypical effort of treating others as you want to be treated. My truth told me that unlike all of them, I was able to juggle and manage everything that was important to me by giving a fair amount of my time and my effort, my love and my appreciation, my attention, and my consideration, equally across the board! No missteps on my part. I had prioritization under control and the rest of the dummies were and are failures. When the reality was, sure I was trying to be equitable is the sharing of myself but that was probably the highest level of self-mismanagement known to the human race. All of it was a lie that I was telling myself and anyone who would listen. I have been filling everyone up from an empty ass cup. I wanted to be first to them because I was making myself last to myself.

This type of self-analysis of behavior, this analysis of similarities in the men that I chose whether it be physical similarities or spiritual similarities, or financial similarities started to tie things together for me. I am choosing these men.

Relationships are Invitation Only.

Basically, I'm saying, "Hey you! Come over here into my life and fuck it up with me!" I'm saying, "Hey! Come over here and pretend like you really want to be with me and then treat me like shit. Just like I treat myself." I'm the one that is inviting that type of energy into my life because that's where I am internally…. that's where I was internally.

I thought the control that I needed to have in my life and in my relationships was external. I get everybody around me to do the thing that I need them to do so I can fill holes and feel whole. So I can feel loved and appreciated. But the reality is life just doesn't work that way.

I was getting back at everyone for things others had done to me. I was punishing people for dying on me, cheating on me, moaning like a little bitch during sex, making me like them even though they were a playboy, not taking initiative, being boring, being white, being married, being sick, having options, being old, being young, taking too long to want to love me the right way, and, abusing me. I was subconsciously getting revenge on people who weren't even thinking about me.

I thought being in control was pretending like everyone was expendable. I didn't need them. They needed me.

I thought I didn't have power anywhere else, so I used my body to take back all I labeled as stolen.

The more I sit down to journal and have conversations with myself about who I am and why I am, I get clearer and clearer. I've spent 40 plus years trying to control this lack of control in my life and if I am going to fix me in hopes of having better relationships, then I am going to have to turn some things around and do some inner work. I am going to have to start lining things up in a way that make it easy to discard things that no longer serve me even if it's my own behavior and belief systems. I'm still working on that! So here I am half-way through my life learning all these lessons. I've finally stopped conning myself and others so that I can truly begin to become aware and also disciplined enough to showcase a healthy method to gaining control of myself, not others.

The rest will fall in line.

That I am sure of.

chapter five

ill[US]ion

*"Your task is not to see
for love, but merely to seek
and find all the barriers
within yourself that you
have built against it."*

- RUMİ

A Second, Ferst

Joye jogged through Piedmont Park with more than fitness and health on her mind this morning. Today she was hoping that someone would notice her hard work. She was beautiful and single, *again* . Forty had come and gone, and her life was a little off-track from the one she had dreamed up for herself. After the run-in with the Black Panther and her bullshit engagement to The Other Frat, she was refocused, relocated, and ready to get back to dating men who could really be contenders in the husband department. Having fun was *fun* but it was time she got serious about rising up in love. Joye hadn't been out on a date since the 26-day love affair. Even though work and life kept her distracted most of the time the thought of her love life was heavy on her mind. Surely, she wasn't undesirable.

Joye was freshly donned in her Puma gear because it showed every cut and curve on her body and because she liked to look fresh when she had an ugly stinky workout.

Joye stopped to take a sip of water. As she looked around the park, she shook her head and chuckled. "What the hell am I doing?" she said out loud to herself as she was thinking about her quest to meet a man while running through the park. A man who ran would at least share her interest in fitness that none of her other exes had shared. She thought to herself *Maybe this is the new thing I'll try?* She turned and walked back in the direction of her apartment.

Joye didn't fantasize about her dream wedding any longer, but she fantasized about her ideal man...quintessential man of every girl's dreams, at least according to fairy tales: tall, dark, handsome, and powerful, whatever that meant.

Another silent thought: *This park is filled with gay men anyway. Idiot! Go home!*

When Joye got back home, her phone rang just as she was searching for something to eat for breakfast. It was her "down for whatever," friend Derek. Whether it was making a midnight Waffle House run, or jumping on an impromptu flight to Jamaica, Derek was ready to go.

"Hey, what's up? How are you?" Derek asked.

With a huge sigh, "I'm fine, Derek. What do you want?"

"Ewww. You sound so disappointed to hear from me? Did you meet someone today?" Derek said sarcastically.

"No. Is that what you called me for? Because if it is you can get off the phone right now."

"Nope. Actually, that's good because I want you to meet someone later on."

"Boy, bye! I'm not going on no damn blind date. Hell no. Blind dates don't work anyway. Haven't you been watching all those shows? *Married at First Sight, Love is Blind*...all statistical failures."

"And running through that very gay park until you can barely breathe doesn't work either. It is the epitome of statistical failures or whatever you wanna call it, yet you do that faithfully every morning. Doncha?"

"Shut. Up."

"Anyway, boo, one of my friend's brothers asked about you. He wants to know if he can get your number?"

"Ha. Ha. Fucking Ha." Joye belted out. 'No."

"Can you be serious for a second? I think you'll like him."

"I am being serious. I don't want to be hooked with some weirdo. You know that's all you know are weirdos. Tell him I said nope, nope, and nope! Thank you. Have a nice day!"

"Please do it for me? I promised him that you would go out with him. Plus, he gave floor seats for the Hawks - Lakers game."

"You sex-trafficked me to your friend's brother, some strange man, for a goddamn basketball ticket? What is happening? Am I being *Punk'd*? Where is Ashton? Chance?"

"Come on. You don't have to have sex with him! Unless you want to. He's really a nice guy. And I made you sound better than Beyonce, hoe. Better than the Queen Bee herself! So, go and have a little fun. You need it. You've been acting like an old hag since your little Marvel-ous boy toy dumped you."

"You are so dumb. Ugh, I cannot believe yo' dumb ass. And I am better than Beyonce, Negro. Why are we even friends?"

"Please, baby, baby, baby, baby, please!"

"Oh my God! Shut up. What's his name?"

"His name is Keith and he's going to caallll yoouuuu right about now! Bye!"

"What?"

Derek hung up the phone. Another call was coming in. Joye rubbed her temples in distress. "Why is he doing this to me?"

She whispered to herself. "Hello?"

"Hello. Is this Joye?"

"Yep."

"Great. My name is Keith. I am a friend of Derek's. Sorta. He, um, he told me that you would be expecting my call?"

"Yes. I just talked to him. Sooo, when are you available to go out on this date that we're supposed to go on?

"Oh, you're getting right to it? Okay. I like that. Well, I was hoping we could go tonight. If that's cool with you."

"Yeah. Yeah. That's fine."

"That's fine? That's it? You don't have any questions you want answered before we go out?"

"Nope. Just pick me up at 7:15." Joye figured that this was a friend of Derek so she could trust him a little bit. "I'll give you my address when you're on the way. Just text me."

"Oh, Derek didn't tell you?"

Joye could feel it in her bones that this was the moment of bullshit. "Tell me what?"

"That I don't have a car. BUT, I am happy to send you a Lyft or an Uber. Whatever you prefer."

"No, he didn't tell me that. But that's okay. I'll drive. So I'll come and pick you up. Is that cool?"

"If it's cool with you it's cool with me. Or I can just meet you wherever we decide to go. I'm not trying to be an inconvenience more than I'm trying to be straight up."

"Nope. It's settled. I'm driving." Joye had a question for Keith, "Do you at least know how to drive?"

"Ahhh, of course, I know how to drive. I just don't own a car right now. I'm new to the city and I live downtown, so I don't really need one with my wor..."

"No need to explain. It's all good. Text me your address, and I will see you at 7:15 on the dot."

"Aiight. Looking forward to it."

Joye was in shock. She walked over to her patio and looked out. She wasn't feeling too good about her love life, her terrible friend, or the breakfast that she never got to eat. She had an apple in her hand. She bit it.

"Am I this desperate?" She continued eating her apple and thought *I wonder what life would be like if Eve's bitch ass had just minded her business and did as she was told? Shit.* She said aloud, "I don't listen either. So..."

Sigh.

Joye turned on her music and turned the volume up real loud, went into the bathroom, grabbed a towel, and jumped in her shower. It was concert time. She got cleaned up and dressed in a crisp white tee and oversized and ragged boyfriend jean shorts. When she propped her foot on the entryway bench to tie her sneakers she was wondering if she would change her clothes for her evening date. She kicked her shoe off and made a dash for her closet. She grabbed a black leather jacket and some heels. She would change into this if she was out too long and unable to make it home to refresh her outfit.

On Saturdays, Joye kept her routine of popping up on her younger sister, Melanie. She had been married to Kyle for 6 years, and they had a gorgeous little girl named Sara who was 3 years old. Joye could hear Melanie in the backyard, so she walked around the house and invited herself in. They were having a little family fun time.

"Heyyy! We didn't know you were stopping by today." Melanie called out.

"You always know I'm stopping by. That is what I do. I stop by on Saturdays." Joye planted kisses on each of them.

"Hey sissy. Hey, Kyle. Hey pretty girl. How are you, you little tootsie pop? Give me some of that sugar." Sara giggled and gave her auntie hugs and kisses. Then she ran back to the trampoline and continued to play.

Kyle asked, "Hey young lady. You staying out of trouble?"

"Tuh. Of course, I am. Why would you ask that? I'ma always be a good girl."

"Yeah, right. Good girl my black ass."

"Please stop cursing around my baby."

Kyle was a pretty solid guy: a great husband for Melanie and a great dad to Sara. They had a good marriage that sometimes appeared to be perfect. They were very close to perfect until they started judging everyone and everything for not being as perfect as they were. As a couples' therapist, Kyle had helped Melanie through a lot of her issues. The girls' mother didn't care for Kyle in the beginning, so that caused a lot of drama in their relationship early on. But their mom never really liked any of their boyfriends. And if she did, Melanie and

Joye definitely broke up with them. Their father didn't care so long as his girls had a smile on their faces. He was more easygoing than the women in the family. He was quiet but very present about the girls choosing a partner. God rest his soul.

"So what's wrong with you?" The therapist in Kyle was in full effect.

Joye crinkled her entire face. "Nothing. Why would something be wrong with me?"

Melanie chimed in before her husband could psycho-analyze her sister. "How's dating going, sis? What's up with your love life?"

"Oh my god! Why is that the question of the damn day?" Joye asked, annoyed that everyone was so zoned in on her relationship status.

Melanie was the younger sister, but she acted like their grandmother. "Because you're not getting any younger, babe. And, you're gonna need a husband sooner than later. I mean, Mom is literally worried about you, especially now since daddy's gone. She's afraid to die because you wouldn't have anyone to look after you. You know what I'm talkin' about?"

"Oh wow. Y'all are some bonafide haters. And your mother needs to stop. For the record, my love life is bone dry as usual! But it's okay. I'm optimistic." Joye kept it light.

"Have you been making yourself available and open to dating again? 'Cause you know you be making faces and turning your nose up. Brothers are not interested in that." Kyle had an opinion about Joye's attitude and presence overall. He would always give her a hard time for being a little bourgeoisie.

"Let me help you out, Bruh! Who said I was only available for the brothers?" Joye was loud, sarcastic, and wrong.

"Well, I didn't necessarily mean Black men. My point is, no man wants a snooty, uppity, chick." Kyle turned to his wife for approval.

"Wait a minute. Maybe you should say men don't want their woman to be snooty and uppity with them. 'Cause they definitely want her to be snooty and uppity with other men. Am I right? Or am I right, dear Dr. Brother-in-Law?"

"Hell yeah. What you being nice to other men for? You ain't got no business smiling up in other men's faces..." They all laughed.

"Leave her alone Kyle. You are ridiculous. We do worry about you, Joye. Not because you need a man or anything like that, but it would be nice to see you being taken care of sometimes."

Joye released a hard sigh, "Oh, how I agree, sis. The stars just haven't aligned for me in that way yet. However, you should know that you and your bubblehead husband aren't the only people looking out for me. Stupid ass Derek set me up on a blind date tonight."

"Tonight? So you're gonna go?" Melanie was surprised.

Joye nodded yes. "And it doesn't sound good. I'm just trying to be open. He sounds broke."

"What kind of shit is that? How does one sound broke?"

Kyle was disappointed in Joye. "I thought you started seeing Dr. Ellis?"

"I don't know if he's broke, I was just saying something to say it. Stop taking everything so literal, doctor man."

"Okay. What about Dr. Ellis? Did you start seeing her yet?"

"I did."

"Good. Stick with it. I'm telling you. You need to do better little girl. She will help you...since you refuse to listen to me!" Kyle was really sick and tired of Joye's antics.

"I know. I'm still going to go on the date. I haven't been on one in so long and anyway, I promised Derek." Joye had no clue of what she was doing. She really didn't want to go on the date, but she had already committed to it.

Instead of harping on the problem, she focused on her sweet niece, Sara. "I just stopped by to see my little tootsie pop." Joye played with Sara for a few hours. They went on a store run to Target and picked up snacks and of course a bunch of things that weren't on the list. Melanie and Kyle prepared a nice early dinner for the family and of course, Joye was invited to dine with them.

"Not sure if you're hungry now or if you're going to wait for your date, but please, stay for dinner." Kyle requested.

"Yayy! Please stay for dinner Auntieeee." Sara was having a ball and enjoying all the attention. Joye agreed. She stayed, even though she didn't eat anything.

"Alright loves. I smell like outside messing around with Sara's little behind. Let me go home and get cleaned up. It's almost that time!" Joye said as she kissed everyone goodbye.

Joye was feeling a little pathetic about the blind date, but it was a little too late to turn back. While she was driving back to her house she was thinking to herself *Girl, you are better than this! Waiting around hoping that someday you'll meet him. What the hell is wrong with you, huh? Letting stupid ass Derek talk you into going out with this fool. You must be smoking crack!*

Joye began daydreaming about the time a co-worker set her up on a blind date when she was younger. The doorbell rang, and when her mom looked through the peephole, and

insisted that no one was there. She walked away. *Ding dong.*
Confused, her mom went back to the door. Still, no one was
there. Well, after the bell rang a third time her mom decided to
open the door. Behold! There was a small man standing there
wearing shorts with tube socks and dress shoes. This is where
internal laughter ensued. Joye was a woman of her word, so
she had her mother ask the gentleman to wait. She stepped out
in good faith with a positive attitude. As they walked to his
car she noticed that it was a raggedy and rusted burnt orange
pickup truck. She almost fell out but kept walking. *One foot in
front of the other, Joye!* is what she kept repeating in her head.
The guy kept talking about his other car being a BMW and ex-
plaining all the reasons why he was driving this horrible vehicle. Joye pretended everything was good. She wanted to hurry
and end the date. He had the nerve to ask for a second date.
All Joye could do was wonder why he thought they had a love
connection.

Joye snapped back to reality.

At her apartment, she looked at her watch and noticed
that she had about an hour to pull it together and get ready
for what she felt would turn out to be a disastrous date. Joye
grabbed the jacket and shoes that she had taken with her earlier and placed them back in her closet neatly. She grabbed a
white shirt dress.

She turned on the music and began playing her 90s playlist that started off with TLC "What About Your Friends." Joye
grabbed fresh towels from the linen closet and jumped into the
shower again. Dancing and lip-syncing every word. Two con-
certs within six hours was impressive.

While she was in the shower her phone rang constantly.

Wet from the shower she grabbed a towel and then checked her voicemail.

"Hey, babe! This is Kema. I'm coming over tonight to see you. So be ready! I'm making this a Girls' Night Out. But just us.

"Okay. Bye!"

"Delete. " Joye said out loud. "I ain't going nowhere with you tonight crazy woman." She looked at the next several messages and said, "Why is he leaving me messages?"

"Joye? It's me, Ferst. I've been trying to reach you for a minute. Can you please return my call when you get this message? I need to talk to you. All right." Joye didn't delete this message.

"Hey. Joye, this is Ferst again. I really need to talk to you. Can you please call me back? Please."

"Joye. Are you okay? I don't usually have this much trouble catching up with you. Uh, maybe you're traveling. Call me back as soon as you get this."

Joye got back to getting dressed. She combed her hair and put on a little bit of makeup. "Let me go and pick this man up."

Right before walking out of her house, she realized that she didn't have her cell phone. She took her shoes off and ran into the bathroom. When she picked up her phone she noticed that she had another missed call and a new voicemail message from Ferst. Even though she thought it was odd for him to blow her up in this way, she ignored him and got back on track, grabbed her keys, her jacket, and left the apartment. She jumped on the elevator and made her way to her car.

She noticed someone was parked next to her with their car running and the headlights glaring. Safety first, she slowed down and reached in her jacket pocket for her mace. But as she got closer and took a better look she knew exactly who it was.

A well-built, very handsome, 6 foot 7-inch God-like man stepped out of the car.

"Rick Fox?!" Joye joked.

"Hahaha. Still funny as ever."

"Ferst? What are you doing here?" Joye was concerned and happy to see me. She gave him a big hug that quickly turned into a church hug.

"I'm sorry for popping up on you like this, but I've been calling you all day. I left like three messages."

"Yeah, I know. But I can't talk to you right now. I'm on my way out." Joye didn't want to be rude but she wanted to make it clear that he did not have "pop up" access or priority in her life.

"Then I'll join you."

"No. Inviting yourself to places? That's a bad idea. I have a date."

"A date? You dating somebody now?"

"Uh, yeah. A date. You trying to tell me you have a problem with me dating?" Joye said playfully. "Anyway, why are you here at my house. What's going on?"

"Everything is going on. But mostly I miss you. And, um, I've been reaching out to you and hoping I can get a chance to talk to you. And I mean really talk to you about us."

As long as Joye had known Ferst, she had never known him to be the type to show up unannounced at any woman's house, job, or anywhere else, so she knew whatever was going on was serious.

"Us? Boy—" Joye went to push past him, but he gently stopped her by grabbing her hand. She turned around and looked at Ferst. He squeezed her hands softly and he could feel her trembling from being just a bit nervous about being so close to him after all this time.

"Just listen, please. I need you to just listen to me. Can I get that?"

"Listen? I always listen to you and that hasn't gotten us any-where. Remember me calling you asking you to listen to me, but you couldn't even get being my friend right?" Joye tried hard not to let her emotions take over but she failed. "Yeah. Whenever you're messing around or got a little girlfriend you act like I don't exist. Ignoring my calls and texts. Now you want me to listen to you. You funny. What do you want me to hear? That you're sorry?"

"Joye, I didn't come here to argue with you. I came to tell you what I want and need, how I've been thinking about you." Ferst pleaded with Joye. "Please? Take a breath and let's talk. Just talk. I just need to talk to you without all of this," Ferst said motioning with both of his hands in a circle. Joye was getting irritated.

"All of this?" Joye rolled her eyes. "I have to go, Ferst. Some-one is waiting for me." Joye turned away and got into her car.

Ferst yelled out, "I'll be here when you get back!"

Joye pulled off. Ferst watched her drive away, then ran a few errands and came back and parked in the same spot.

He had all night, and he was prepared to wait.

෯

Blind Dating

Joye parked in front of Keith's house. He lived in a cute bungalow in the Grant Park area of the city. She looked at the

GPS and then checked her text message to make sure she had the right location.

Joye proceeded to walk to the front door of the house. When she looked down at her watch it was 8:45 p.m.; she was really late. Keith opened the door and said, "You've got to be Joye!"

"Keith? Hi. Yes, I'm sorry."

He said, "I thought you changed your mind for a second."

"I am truly sorry for being late. Something important popped up at the last minute."

"Well, come in. Please."

Keith led Joye through his house to the den area where they sat on the couch. Keith was average looking to Joye. She didn't have any immediate attraction to him. His house was nicely decorated though and seemed to have a touch of old-school flavor in it. She felt out of place.

"I don't expect you to really want to drive around tonight, so if you want we can just order something and chill here at the house. We can talk, watch some Netflix. Whatever you want."

"Well, what do you want to do?" Joye's mind was somewhere else. She was thinking about Ferst standing in her parking garage looking crazy.

Keith blurted out, "Let's order Vietnamese. You like pho and banh mi?" He pronounced both food choices all the way wrong. He said, "foe" and "band me."

"What!?" Joye was mad at first but then she realized how funny it was and giggled. "Yeah. All of that's fine."

Keith was confused about why she was laughing at him but ignored it. He pulled up an Uber Eats app and began scrolling through until he found a pretty decent Vietnamese restaurant that would deliver within 30 minutes.

Keith engaged Joye in some major small talk. Joye talked about her consulting business, and Keith explained exactly what he did as a mobile marketing and development manager for the Atlanta Hawks.

Joye interrupted him by saying, "Seems like a cool job! Is that how you got those Lakers tickets for Derek?"

Keith was embarrassed that she knew how he bought this date with her. "He told you about that? That boy is crazy."

"Yeah, he did. He's a good friend. He just tries to look out for me. Ya know?"

Without thinking, Keith responded, "Yeah he told me you couldn't get a date! Hell, I can't get one either, so I thought I'd do whatever necessary to have a nice night with a beautiful girl."

"Wow. He told you that I couldn't get a date?"

Laughing, "Yeah. He was telling me about how you jog through the park trying to chase men down. I told my mother when she came home about it yesterday, and she was rolling."

Joye looked at Keith like he was completely insane. She was offended. Just when she got ready to say something the door-bell rang, and Keith jumped up to answer it. She assumed it was their dinner. Keith opened the door and announced that it was his mother. She had bags of groceries.

Keith's mom was a traditional old school grandmother, not one of these fly grandmothers of today. Joye could see and hear them talking from the den.

"Boy, you still up making noise? Help me put these grocer-ies in the kitchen."

"Mom. I have company."

"I don't care; tell them fools to come and help too. It's a lot more stuff to be brought in."

"Mom! It's my date."

"A date? Is that the desperate girl that runs through the park stalking men? That girl's got a problem. I don't know if you want to have her up in my house. She may be some type of *Fatal Attraction* girl. Can't be too trusting nowadays."

Joye was so humiliated. She got up and found her way to the kitchen where Keith and his mother were unpacking groceries and said hello. Joye reached over to help his mother with the bags.

"How you doing, baby?" Ms. Thompson asked Joye.

"Oh, I've been better ma'am. Trust me."

"Well you just keep on and God will send you somebody special. Someone you deserve. But I don't think it's safe for you to be walking the park all day searching for a man, though. Not in these times. There's too many racists and rapists and just weirdos all around this city."

"I'm sorry, ma'am. That is not accurate. I don't chase men through the park."

"Are you calling my baby a liar?"

"Oh my God! Mom! Can you please be quiet?"

"It's okay, Keith. I think it's time for me to go anyway," Joye said.

"But we haven't done anything yet? The food's not even here!"

"Just let her go, baby. It's never worth crying over spilled or spoiled milk."

Joye thought to herself *"Did this muthafucka just call me spoiled milk? Old bitch!"*

Joye showed herself out.

Keith followed her begging and apologizing about how things turned out. Joye ignored him and threw up her hands, while Keith went back into his house and yelled at his mother.

⚭

Still, Ferst

When Joye returned to her apartment Ferst was still waiting inside of his car. He told her he would be there when she returned, and he was. Ferst was working double-time at doing what he said he would because he had finally begun to realize how important that is for Joye. He hurried to exit his vehicle and helped her get out of her car.

Joye was flattered that Ferst had waited for her. "You know you are crazy right?"

"Yes, I know. That's why you fell in love with me."

"Ahh. Yes. Fell. The operative word. Hmm. Past tense."

"Woman, you're killing me. Are you going to talk to me this time instead of screaming and ignoring me and then running away?"

Joye was reluctant, but she recognized he was serious, and she wasn't going to completely shut him down. "First of all, I never screamed, ignored, or ran away. But yeah, we can talk. Do you want to come upstairs?" She was playing the tough girl. Ferst wasn't fooled.

Ferst followed Joye onto the elevator. She made it a point to stand as far away from him as she could. She was trying to be on her best behavior.

"Hey? Why did you come back so quick? Was your date that bad?"

Joye wanted to say "mind your business" but she also wanted to talk shit about her terrible blind date. "Oh, man, was it? After his mother came in and started talking all types of crap about me I just left. I didn't even eat."

"His mother?" They both laughed. "So let me cook for you?"

"It's too late. Plus, I need to grocery shop. Don't tell me? You have groceries in the car?" Ferst just winked at her and shrugged as if to say, "maybe I do." Joye opened the door and Ferst made his way towards the kitchen.

"Wash your damn hands, boy!" Joye yelled out.

"Oops. I forgot you're a germaphobe." Ferst looked down and kicked his shoes off before she noticed he had walked on her floors with his street feet.

"Oh!? I didn't tell you, but Shade is here with me" Shade was a puppy that Ferst had bought for Joye several years ago right before they finally broke up. He was a brown Havanese. Joye didn't want to keep the dog when he left, but she certainly loved him.

"Really? I just assumed he was —." Joye made a face because her thought was morbid.

"Nah. He is still kickin'. He's at doggy daycare. I needed a few days to run around. It's been very hectic since getting into town. But I'll grab him in a couple of days."

"He's still healthy? How old is he now?"

"Yes, he's healthy; he's just old. He's fifteen." Saying he was fifteen triggered an emotion in Ferst. Joye saw the look on his face and said with a confronting tone, "Yup, it's been that long, Ferst."

Ferst started looking through Joye's cabinets to see what he could conjure up. She must have lied about needing to go to the grocery store earlier because her cabinets and refrigerator were packed with all kinds of food.

Ferst decided on a grilled cheese sandwich.

Joye went to her room and changed into her comfy clothes which for her were boy shorts and an oversized hoodie. Ferst immediately recognized the hoodie and wondered if she had worn it on purpose.

"I have been looking for my hoodie for years!"

"Oh yeah? This right here—is mines!" Joye joked in her worst California west coast accent.

Joye plopped down on the couch and Ferst served her dinner.

"Here you go, ma'am. Dinner is served. " Ferst presented the sandwich and made hand gestures like he was a garcon in some 5-star restaurant.

"They're burnt."

"They're blackened. Cajun grilled cheese. Are you really that uncultured?"

"You stupid." Joye just looked at him and laughed. She scraped the Cajun off her sandwich, but she still ate it. "Anyway, Ferst. What's going on with you? Why are you creeping around my house, leaving back to back messages like a weirdo? Is everything okay?"

"Well," Ferst sat on the couch next to her. "Everything's not okay but most things are great. Honestly, I have just been thinking about us and where I am in my life and where you are in yours and," He held his breath for a second then said, "I just don't understand why you're not my wife."

"Your wife?" Joye pretended to choke on her sandwich. "Oh, that's what we doing now? You taking big leaps."

"Yes, my wife. I know you're not surprised. I love you. I always have. And, I know that you love me. Don't you think it's time to stop pretending like we're gonna find what we want and have in each other in someone else? I mean, I've tried, and I've failed. You've tried. Shit, you tried tonight, and look what happened. The Gods placed your ass right back in my arms which is where you belong?" Ferst grabbed Joye's calf and softly shook it in a joking manner.

"I cannot deal with you. All of these years pass by and now you think it's the right time, why?" Joye was genuinely surprised by this conversation.

"Why not? I grew up! I'm a better man now. I know you have reservations about our past and some of the things that happened between us, but I'm telling you I am not that guy anymore. I will never ever hurt you in that way again. I just need you to believe me. And trust me. I want you to consider a life together with me. The right way. No bullshit this time." They stared at each other for a brief moment.

Joye put her plate on the coffee table and sat up straight on the couch.

"Ferst, I hate that you're asking me this now. This is so delayed and so random. I do want to believe you. I just don't know that this is the right thing to do. I definitely am uncertain about doing it right now."

Joye was feeling anxious.

She stood up and folded both her arms over the top of her head. She took a few steps then turned around and continued, "I mean you really destroyed me and I'm not ready to act like you didn't. To ask me to consider us being together in a real way is a lot for me. Every now and again I get a glimpse of all the reasons why we didn't work. I still get angry about it. *All of it.*"

Ferst stood up and walked over to Joye and softly pinched her chin. "Joye 'No Middle Name' Allyn? Do you love me?"

"Of course I do. You know that. If I didn't, what happened between us would mean nothing."

"So. It's simple." Ferst threw his hands up as if he won a prize. "If you love me, just think about it."

Joye sighed, "I guess I can do that. You do know that I need more than your love?"

"I do. I plan on giving it to you."

Joye and Ferst made frivolous conversation as she nibbled on the sandwiches he prepared. She really wasn't ready to discuss her feelings with him. Deep down she really cared about him and wanted them to work very badly. But she still felt betrayed by him and did not want to put her heart on the line. Ferst was thankful to be able to sit with Joye and give her a moment to decide if she missed him too.

Joye stared lovingly at Ferst for a minute before she began cleaning the small mess they had made.

"I'm gonna need some water! Ol' dry ass sandwich," she teased.

"Stop hating on my cooking. You know I'm the real deal. I just had an off night tonight. I'm not familiar with this new fancy stove you have. You consultants are rich!"

"Oh, shut up!" Joye handed Ferst a glass of water. "You were definitely the king of the kitchen. Remember that gumbo you made for me and Kema that one time? Oh my god. It was so good. She still talks about that today. That's what you should have made tonight!"

"Woman, I did not have enough time to make gumbo! And you don't have the proper ingredients. But I will make you some, next time."

"What time is it?" Joye reminded Ferst that it was getting late and that he needed to head out. As Ferst was leaving Joye asked him about his parents, in particular his father. She was really cool with him back in the day.

"Man, they are great! They are actually planning their second wedding." Ferst remembered that Joye had lost her father a few years ago. "You know, I'm really sorry about Pop Allyn. I know that was tough for you and the family." Joye's eyes welled up with tears. She immediately held her head in her hand and began to cry.

Ferst wasted no time holding her. "I'm sorry I wasn't there for you. I should have been here for you." She gathered herself quickly and pulled away.

"It's okay. I'm sorry," Joye said, wiping away tears.

"No. Don't apologize. I'm here now. I got you. Whatever you need."

Ferst changed the subject by promising to keep her informed on any of the updates about his parents' pending nuptial renewal and he begged her to get some sleep.

"I'll be checking in with you real soon." Before walking out Ferst leaned in for a kiss but Joye moved. They ended up in an awkward dance as he tried to place a kiss on her cheek. "Girl, let me kiss you!"

Joye laughed, "You're a whole idiot. Bye!"

Joye watched Ferst walk down the hall and toward the elevator. She thought to herself *How in the world was I able to control myself?* She waved goodbye and closed the door. Ferst left a lot on her mind with the proposition he put on the table.

She was thinking, *His wife?*

೪

Joye climbed into bed. She wasn't really tired, but she had nothing else to do that night. She was already dressed to relax and she damn sure wasn't getting up to go out with Kema. Right before she turned off her lights her phone rang. It was Kema.

Kema had been trying to reach her all day as well. She was asking her if she was going to hang out with her tonight.

"Kema the only reason you want me to go out tonight is so you can drink, and I can drive."

"No! That's not the only reason. I know you need to get out of the house too."

"Kema I've been out of the house already twice today. Now I'm back, and I'm staying right here."

"Really? Where the hell did you go?"

"You know I went to my sister's to see my niece. Then I went on a stupid blind date with some loser that Derek hooked me up with. It was horrible."

"Why are you so crazy? You know you don't go nowhere with anybody Derek knows! What happened?"

"The short is he lives at home with his mama. He's short. I wasn't attracted to him at all. And he paid to go out on a date with me. Shall I continue?"

"Yikes. Girl, it sounds like you had a rough night. That's all the more reason for you to come out with me."

"Nope. Guess who just left here? Ferst."

"Oh, I love him. How is he? I know he's still fine! Wait a minute? Why do you always have 100 niggas around you at one time? Did you give him some ass?"

"Oh, Jesus. No. He's good. And, hell yeah he is still fine. He wanted to talk about getting back together like together, together. Like marriage, together."

"What? Wow! Well, Joye, maybe he learned from his mistakes. It's been such a long time, and I mean, you love this man. Maybe you need to think about it. I mean, if he's talking grown man talk it might be worth listening to, unlike that other guy that was talking that talk and was obviously playing games."

"Yeah. I'm going to think about it. I'm just not sure I'm ready. Anyway, I'm not going out with you so enjoy the night and be safe, please. I'm tired. I'm going to get some rest."

"Tired? Only one thing you could be tired from at this time of the night. I know you gave him some ass. Bye hoe!"

It was 12:43 a.m., and Joye couldn't fall asleep fast enough. She kept thinking about her encounter with Ferst tonight. She was open to revisiting the relationship. She just didn't want to put down her guard yet. She was also thinking about what Kema said about giving up the ass. She laughed to herself because that thought had definitely crossed her mind.

She assumed that Ferst must be doing okay in life and in business because he was looking better than ever before. Joye couldn't help but reflect on how great he looked. It was 1:41 a.m. *Damn it!* she thought to herself. She had spent a whole hour just thinking about a man.

She forced herself to go to sleep.

❦

The sun was shining in on Joye's face. She tossed and turned knowing that she should get up, but her bed was so comfortable. She squinted her eyes to see what time it was. It was 10 o'clock. She had overslept. She missed her morning jog.

Joye couldn't remember the last time she had fallen off schedule. She took so much pride in her organizational skills. She had her life patterns down to a "T." Everything was based around a schedule but since Ferst had shown up unexpectedly last night she had been late twice.

She threw the sheet off of her and sat on the edge of her bed.

"Oh, well." she blurted out as she thought about missing her normal routine. She still decided to take her jog through Piedmont Park. She had become obsessed with staying healthy and keeping her body intact. She was doing a great job. After a good hour and a half workout, she made her way back home.

When Joye arrived at the front of her building Ferst was driving up to surprise her. He pulled over as soon as he saw an available parking space and jumped out of the car.

He stopped by the kennel a little earlier than expected and picked up Shade. Joye noticed the dog first.

"Hi, Shade! Hiiii." Joye began rubbing and petting Shade.

"Girl, you speaking to the dog before you speak to me?"

"Well, I saw you a few hours ago. Good morning, though," Joye said with a bite. Ferst leaned in and kissed her on the cheek. Joye didn't respond to his kiss and picked up Shade. "But I haven't seen my dog in years. What's up, poo pah? He treating you okay?" Shade was excited and playful.

"Oh, now he's your dog? You ain't shit, Joye." Ferst could not believe she was questioning his caretaker skills. "I should have given you the name Shade and not the dog."

"Ferst? What are you doing here? You really are on some creepy stalker*ish*."

"Do I look like a creepy stalker? I'm way too fly for that."

"Ewww. Gross." Joye hated it when he acted arrogantly and only focused on how he looked. "You're one of the smartest men I know, but you're always talking about being 'cute' and acting stupid. Just sad."

"Sound fa-MIRROR?" Ferst playfully got in Joye's face and looked her in her eyes. They had a lot more in common than she was willing to admit.

"Whatever."

"I was about to go grab lunch. You wanna roll?"

"Aww, man. That's right. It's after 12 o'clock. I woke up late." Joye's muscles were tensing up. She hadn't stretched from her run yet. She pulled her legs to her backside, tilting her head left and right.

"Why don't you let me run you a hot bubble bath for your muscles then take you to lunch?"

Joye remembered how sweet Ferst could be at times. She wanted to say no but how could she refuse him?

"I don't know about running me a bath, but lunch? If you're treatin', I'm eatin'." They laughed and headed upstairs to her place.

Ferst looked down at Shade as they entered the building and gave him the power fist. "Good dog." He knew that if Joye had an adverse reaction to seeing Shade she would have sent him and the dog away.

Joye was trying to open her house door but dropped her water bottle and earbuds. Ferst immediately lowered down to pick them up. He was on one knee with his hand raised up toward her. She just looked at him with the *are you dumb?* face.

"You want my arm to fall off?"

Joye rolled her eyes, "Yes, Billy Dee. I want your arm to fall off."

Joye opened her door and walked in, Ferst walked in right behind her and he accidentally closed the door on the dog.

"Don't leave him out there! Hell, if you can come in he can definitely come in."

"Oh shit. My bad, Shade. Sorry man."

"Okay. I'm gonna take a shower. Give me 20 minutes?"

"Twenty minutes?"

"Yes! I'll hurry." Joye acknowledged the dog. "Are you leaving him or is he coming with us?"

"Doesn't matter. He can stay if you don't mind. He doesn't have to eat for a few more hours."

"Cool. He can stay if he isn't going to tear up my house."

"Nah. He won't do that. He is super chill."

Joye went into her room, closed the door, and got her playlist ready for her shower. She mumbled, "I thought you were gonna run me a hot bubble bath?"

After Ferst found a bowl and gave Shade fresh water, he sat on the couch. Looking around he just marveled at how she never forfeited the opportunity to keep her space beautiful and clean.

Ferst felt at home.

He got up to peek around the house a bit more and came across a wooden picture box under one of the end tables. It was filled with pictures of Joye as a teenager, pictures of her parents, her sister, and Kyle at their wedding. There were also pictures of her with her niece and some with her girlfriends.

She had photos of her with colleagues on business trips. At the very bottom of that box, Ferst found a picture of a tiny baby's footprint and vial. Then underneath that a picture of him and Joye at an amusement park. Ferst tucked the box back where he found it.

Joye walked out and asked, "What are you doing?"

Ferst turned around and admired how pretty and young she looked. She looked at him waiting for an answer but Ferst looked at his watch. He was amazed that she was able to pull herself together within twenty minutes, as promised. She had a long pale pink skirt that fit her body just enough to see the curves and an ivory mid-sleeve half t-shirt. With very little makeup on she was still a natural beauty.

Ferst snapped out of his daze, "Oh, I was just looking at old photos." He quickly changed the subject, "You look beautiful by the way."

Joye flirtatiously said, "Thanks. Did I take too long?"

"Nope. You're right on time. Let's go."

"Do you want me to drive?"

"No. My car is right up front, remember?"

"Where is Shade? He's on the patio. He is safe with water and I found some gadgets for him to play with."

Joye had a look on her face that screamed *that's not a good idea*, but she was trying to complain less, so she said absolutely nothing. Her face spoke volumes though. She was also wondering *Where the hell did you find gadgets for a dog in my house?*

Ferst assured Joye that Shade was going to be okay on the patio. "He's a punk dog, Joye. He ain't going nowhere. Scary ass dog." He softly poked Joye on the side of her waist and said, "Just like his mama."

"I am so over you already."

"Already? We're just getting started."

In the elevator, Joye was standing much closer to Ferst than the night before. Ferst loaded her up with compliments. She was comfortably uncomfortable because she didn't really like too many compliments.

Ferst opened the passenger door for her. "Oh! That's new. You took classes on chivalry and being a gentleman?"

"You bleed ice-cold water don't you, Joye? Damn. Just give me my props and say 'thank you baby'," Ferst got in the driver's seat. "We're going to make a quick stop before we eat. I want to show you something. Is that cool?"

"If I say no?"

"You won't say no to me. Not about this."

They drove for about fifteen minutes into a neighborhood called Tuxedo Park. Ferst pulled into a long driveway. There was some construction and grounds work going on at the house. There were also a few movers unloading furniture.

"What's this?" Joye asked.

"It's official. I'm a Georgia resident now."

"This is yours?"

Ferst nodded yes.

"Oh, wow. Ferst. That's awesome. Congratulations. This house is everything and it's not even complete. Jesus."

Ferst smiled, "You like it?"

"I love it so far." Joye looked at Ferst with pride in her eyes. "You're really here now? For good?"

"Well, part-time for now."

Joye was happy but unnerved for some reason. "Why'd you bring me here?" Joye was smart. She knew that Ferst was laying it on thick with an attempt to make it almost impossible for her to deny him. Joye's initial response showed in her body language which equated to why now?

"I wanted to share the good news with you." Ferst was feeling discouraged but wasn't ready to quit. "Joye, I'm probably doing this all wrong, but I am serious about what I asked you last night. This is part of how I want to show you that I am all in. You like structure. You need a foundation. For a long time, I couldn't give you any of that."

Joye interrupted him, "Yeah, because you—"

"Forget the reasons why okay? I'm clear about my choices. I've done my time for everything I did to hurt you *and* things that weren't even my fault. Things that were no one's fault, okay? What do I have to do to get you to take these shackles off of me? Huh?" Ferst was frustrated and didn't understand why he had to fight so hard.

"I'm sorry. I'm just not over all of it yet."

"Well, do what you need to do to get over it. I'm here. Let's figure it out over lunch, alright?" Ferst patted her on her thigh.

Joye was overwhelmed. She had never experienced this deliberate side of Ferst. He was determined and focused, and she was not used to that from him. In their last life together he was scattered and aloof. Just letting life happen day by day and never thinking about the consequences of not planning a future.

Ferst took Joye to Tassili's Raw Reality Cafe in the West End. The food was healthy and tasty. It was also better aligned with her lifestyle than the grilled cheese he had made last night. They ordered and sat outside to enjoy the sun. Joye had the punany wrap and Ferst ordered the mandingo wrap: very appropriate choices for them.

Joye was tired of shuffling around her thoughts. She dove right in. "Tell me about your son."

She said it.

The part of Ferst and Joye that ended them was exactly what she wanted to talk about. Over the years Ferst had only mentioned his son very casually when they would talk and Joye never asked about him. She met him once when he was about two years old.

"He's doing okay. Um, you know he's fourteen now. I still don't get to see him as often as I'd like because you know, his mom is still the same. Um, but he's doing alright." It was tough for Ferst to talk about points of disharmony in his life. However, they both knew that it was time.

"How often do you see him?"

"I try to see him at least once a month. That works most of the time if there's no beef with Aubrii. Ya know, he's pretty athletic so I've been making it to as many games as possible whenever he has them. I'm sure that's going to pick up soon now that he's a sophomore."

"What is he playing, basketball?" Joye wanted to know everything but she kept the questions simple.

"No! Can you believe it? He's a baseballer. Left fielder." Ferst was very proud that his son was athletic. Ferst was a basketball star in college but that dream ended when he shattered his knee. "He's athletic like his father. And he's good too. I got a little classic Bo Jackson on my hands."

"That's dope. So, how do you like being a daddy?" Joye kept digging.

"I take it seriously. I would love it better if I had more access to him and could really wrap my hands around him. But it's been cool." Ferst took a bite of his wrap and looked around contemplating his answer. "It's nothing like how I imagined it would be especially had I done it in a better way. But I love that kid. He's a good kid and I'm gonna keep doing right by him."

"Absolutely." Joye was happy for Ferst but had some feelings of jealousy. She asked, "So no other babies?"

"Nope! No other babies. I don't know how, but—"

"Oh god, spare me." Joye cringed at the thought of him having unprotected sex with other women.

"I'm just saying, I haven't always been safe. That's a fact. And, luckily, I don't have any consequences for my reckless behavior. So, nope. No other babies. I mean, unless you want one?"

Joye chuckled. "Man, you know I wanted at least two. But.."

Ferst interrupted her, "It just wasn't in the cards."

"Yeah. I guess that's a way to look at it." Joye lost her appetite and began picking at her food.

"Hey. Hey. That was a tough loss for both of us, Joye. And it wasn't our fault. Please tell me you're not still beating yourself up over that?"

Joye looked up from her plate, "Is that what you want to hear?"

"Only if it's true."

ॐ

Trauma Ties

Joye and Ferst suffered a miscarriage early in their relationship. Ferst was ecstatic about her pregnancy. Everything was perfect between them. One day Joye called him and told him he needed to get to Atlanta. She was frantic. She was nervous, but she assured him that it was not bad news. Ferst jumped on that plane so quickly. He couldn't even imagine what happened and why she needed him there, right then. Not tomorrow, it had to be that day

Ferst's flight landed after 10:00 p.m. It was October 19th, a date he would never forget. Joye told him to meet her at her house immediately after landing. She said, "Babe, don't stop for food. Nothing. Just come straight here!" Of course, he was concerned that he wouldn't make it on time trying to navigate through that big ass airport. However, he did exactly as she had asked. When Ferst got to the front door of her house she was literally standing in the doorway. She was glowing, but she had a hint of fear in her eyes. As soon as Ferst looked at her he knew.

Joye was pregnant.

She wasn't afraid of being a mom though. That was something she wanted more than anything. She was fearful about the relationship. She wanted Ferst to talk her through what this meant for them and how they would make it work as a couple.

At that time, Ferst had no desire to move, and Joye was still in the thick of becoming independent and building her career. Ferst didn't have a real answer, but he promised Joye that he would be there as often as he could afford. And, he did a terrible job at convincing her to move to the West Coast with him.

Ferst stayed with Joye for over a month that trip. He had already planned to spend Thanksgiving with her, so it wasn't too much of a task to make the adjustment. Joye wanted Ferst to go to her next doctor's appointment and run errands for her. She was already taking advantage of the foot and back rubs. She was entering her third month, her first trimester. The books they read said that's the perfect time to share the good news with friends and family because you're in the safe zone. That Thanksgiving when her family blessed the food, Ferst asked to make a toast. Without Joye's permission, Ferst announced to every person in that house that they were expecting a child.

Ferst was excited.

Joye was terrified.

Ferst was excited because he was a young man on the come up and had a banging ass chick in the South doing her thing. He was hoping to build a foundation toward a life with her, and now they were about to bring an outstanding addition to humanity.

You couldn't tell him shit.

Ferst felt like he was the king of the world.

But Joye felt unsure and embarrassed about her new baby out of wedlock.

Her family was concerned at first, but they soon shared their happiness after Ferst's abrupt announcement. Joye knew her family would respond in that way. Ferst didn't even think it through. It wasn't that they weren't happy for them. They had the same concerns that Joye did: *How are they going to raise a child together if they live so far apart?*

It was a valid question.

Ferst thought he was Superman and Batman and every other superhero back then. He was certain he could figure it out but neither of them knew how.

It turned out that God and the Universe didn't need them to figure out anything.

Joye was seven months pregnant when she lost their baby.

One day she woke and there was blood everywhere. No pain, just blood. She recounted the minutes, hours, days and weeks leading up to that moment in hopes to determine why this happened, but there was nothing out of the ordinary. The doctors maintained that she was perfectly healthy. They didn't detect any abnormalities with the fetus after conducting the autopsy either. They encouraged Ferst and Joye to try again.

Joye called Ferst as soon as she noticed the blood. He was in Florida and tried to convince her to call an ambulance, but she only lived few blocks from the hospital, so she drove herself.

Joye was alone.

Ferst wasn't as lucky on February 16th as he was on October 19th. He could not get a same day flight to save his or their baby's life. Ferst was in Miami at the fucking international boat show. For a long time that simple detail haunted their thoughts. *Why was he at a fucking boat show?* Ferst could never answer that question and Joye beat him up about it for years. Regardless of the reason, Ferst couldn't get a flight from Miami to Atlanta on the same night so he stayed in the airport until he could catch a standby on the next one. He didn't arrive until the following day, and when he landed he darted straight to Emory Hospital.

That was one of the worst days of their lives. Joye lay in that hospital bed looking defeated. No baby. Just two young childless would-be parents in a cold soulless hospital room. Ferst felt powerless. There was nothing he could do.

When Ferst touched her, he could feel her emptiness. She wept and held onto him saying, "We had a daughter." That shattered Ferst's heart into a million pieces. Ferst had asked her not to tell him the baby's gender. He wanted to be surprised in the delivery room. This is not what either of them had in mind.

It was a tragedy. The whole process was traumatic. Joye didn't want to make any decisions about the burial or cremation offered by the hospital without Ferst. So that's what they did that day. They made funeral arrangements for their baby girl.

Between crying and trying to understand, the hospital allowed them to see her one last time. They stood praying and asking for forgiveness for something they may or may not have done to cause this over their dead baby.

Ferst stayed in Atlanta with Joye for almost three months after this incident. Joye finally went on to feel more like herself again. Ferst bought her a puppy to keep her company when he had to head home but she refused him.

ॐ

Ferst Amendments

Joye and Ferst were talking and holding hands at the table at this point.

"I do beat myself up sometimes. It's just sad. I used to dream about being a mother way more than I dreamt of being your wife." Joye said with a tinge of sarcasm. "So it's hard sometimes, especially not having any version of that vision of my family."

Ferst used to think God punished him for his arrogance and ignorance at the time, but he didn't mention that Joye, not then. Instead, he just rubbed Joye's hand and said, "You would have made a wonderful mother. And you still have time. I mean, all of my parts work just fine if you want to test drive."

They both smiled. "Oh, boy. You are so ridiculous. How do

you know they still work? You just said you haven't made any more babies?"

"I'm just saying. I know."

"Well, I don't know. The doctors always say there's nothing wrong. Even now at 40-something, they are still saying I can get pregnant. But I haven't. I have been very careful, but like you—since we're being honest—I have not been safe 100% of the time. I guess you're right, it just wasn't in the cards for me to be a mommy."

"At that time." Ferst wanted to drive his point that he would still give her a baby. "Hey, I never showed you this, but I did something about a year ago. Look at this." Ferst raised up his right sleeve to reveal an elaborate tattoo in honor of their baby girl on his forearm.

"Wow! Joye rubbed her fingers across the tattoo. "Journee." That's amazing."

"Do you like it?"

"I love it. I can't believe you have a tattoo!"

"Look closer." Ferst wanted Joye to see their names were inscribed on the tattoo as well.

"Oh, no! That's wild. Wow!"

"I'm glad you like it. It's one thing to carry y'all in my heart but..."

Joye stopped him, "Ferst?

"Yeah?"

"I'm sorry too. I don't remember ever allowing you to grieve. That was your time too and I made it all about me. I'm sorry I did that to you. I shouldn't have been so selfish."

"No. You were exactly what you needed to be. Don't apologize. You literally carried the brunt of our loss. You don't owe me a damn thing. Not even that I'm sorry. I won't accept it. Do you understand?"

"I do. Thank you."

"Well, you know, I'm willing to try to get you pregnant again if you want."

"You're such an idiot. And you jinxed us by putting my name in that tattoo. You know how that always turns out!"

"Nah, I don't believe in that crap. You and I? We are going to be great."

Joye wanted to shift gears. "Tell me about this part-time move to Atlanta."

"Joye! This shit is aligning perfectly. So, all of my film projects have been taking off like crazy over the last ten years. The documentaries, the shorts, the independent stuff. I'm talking awards: Sundance, LACA, Global, South by Southwest... We got a couple of them. I got a few IMDb credits. It has been unbelievable. You know, with Netflix, Hulu, Apple TV, and even some of the prime networks incessantly looking for new talent, new scripts, new work, in general. We've been able to pitch dozens of ideas and get them sold. So, I've been able to expand my studios." Ferst was really excited.

"That's big. So Ferst Take Studios has a new home in Atlanta? Should I call Tyler Perry and tell him to pack his shit up? That his time's up?" Joye joked.

Ferst laughed, "Hell nah! He made room for me, so I'm gonna let him stay." Ferst continued, "So, yeah that's what's happening with me. Atlanta's pretty much the epicenter of the film industry now. It just made sense to set up shop here too. I wanted to take advantage of the opportunity while I could. That's why I am part-time for now. We'll see how it goes. And, of course, the other reason is my brilliant and most beautiful-est baby is here. Since I could barely get you to come visit the West Coast I decided to come get my woman."

"Oh! Is that right? Whatever. This is so exciting. I'm very proud of you. I know you worked really hard. And you're kinda good at it."

"Kinda? You trippin'! I am the greatest alive!!" Ferst asked a lady sitting at a nearby table to testify, "Ma'am? Tell her. Tell her I'm the greatest alive, please."

"Would you leave people alone? I'm so sorry ma'am."

"Honey he sure does sound like he is the greatest! So maybe he is." The woman winked at Joye and smiled.

"Thank you, ma'am! See. Somebody out here paying attention to your man!" Ferst was making a scene. "Baby, we have so much to talk about but I gotta get back to the house and then over to the office to do a walkthrough of the sets. Let me take you home."

They had a good time laughing all the way back to Joye's place. They always had the best car rides together and enjoyed singing and talking shit to each other.

"So, future wife? Can I have dinner with you tonight?"

"Sir?! Are you asking me for a date?"

"Girl, ask? I don't ask for dates. I *been* dating you since I showed up in your garage."

"You know you sound like a psychopath, right? Why do I even bother with you?"

"I don't care. You can call me asking you to dinner tonight whatever you wanna call it. I'm just trying to give you the new and improved Ferst, and make sure I'm your very last."

"Oh my god. Let me out of this car."

"Is that a yes?"

"Yes."

"Hold on, young lady. I need to come upstairs and grab my dog. Oh, and let me get your door for you."

"How long are you going to keep this up?"

"O! Ye, woman, of little faith."

"I'll bring him down for you." Joye made a dash for the door. About 6 minutes later she came down holding Shade. She had a strange look on her face.

"Here you go. He didn't pee or poop."

Ferst took Shade from her. "He's a good dog. I shall see you in the eve?" Before Joye could answer Ferst asked her if she was okay.

"No, but I'll be fine. And, yes, you can see me later. I just don't want to go out. Can we chill here at my place?"

"Whatever you wish, Lady Allyn."

Joye initiated the hug and the kiss this time. She planted it right on his left cheek and whispered in his ear, "Thank you for today."

"You're welcome. Text me when you get inside."

Joye's stroll into her building and up the elevator seemed like forever. It was like her body was moving in slow motion, but her mind was racing full speed ahead. She was an emotional mess. Ferst was too. They had only scratched the surface of their losses during lunch, but it was more than enough to open up old wounds. As Joye walked to her door she couldn't contain herself any longer and burst into tears. She opened the door and continued to sob.

She hadn't spoken of Journee by name in years. Their daughter would have turned 15 years old this year.

Joye wasn't alone. When Ferst got back into his car he sat for a moment shedding tears too. He also hadn't processed what the pain felt like for either of them in a very long time. While this was probably a necessary conversation it was not easy.

Joye: I'm in.
Ferst: Cool. I'm gone. See you tonight.

☙

Joye had fallen asleep on her couch and was awakened by her cell phone pinging.

Ro: Bitch. Why can't I get a hold of you?
Kema: She must be laid up with Ferst. 🌮
Ro: Ferst? WHAAAT???!!
Ro: Wait? What does the taco emoji mean??? LOL
Kema: Oh she ain't tell you?
Ro: No. Is he back? You know I love me some Ferst.
Kema: I dunno if he's back, back. But he's BACK.
Ro: Good. This might be perfect. Joye? Where are you with the tea, boo?
Kema: I'm telling you she is laid up.
Joye: Both of y'all dumb AF. I am not laid up. I just took a nap. ALONE.
Ro: A nap? This old lady talk is buggin' me out. Like frfr. You're only 42 dude. Why you so tired all of a sudden?
Kema: From laying up I'm sure.

Joye: Idiots

Joye: There has been no laying up for me. Sorry.

Ro: So is it true? Is our man, Ferst, back? I missed him so!!!

Joye: LOL. He is poking his beautiful neck out for me.

Ro: Yay!!!!! Be nice to him. It takes a lot of courage to come back.

Joye: I have been. The last couple of days have been unbelievable. It's just a lot. I need to work through it all. But I have enjoyed him.

Kema: Aww. I love Joye in love. You're always so much better. LOL

Joye: Hush.

Joye: We spoke about Journee

Ro: Oh, Joye. How are you feeling?

Kema: Sheesh. Y'all are getting heavy. Are you okay?

Joye: He has a tattoo of her name and our names on his right arm. It's gorgeous. I just can't process it all...

Joye: I'm okay though. It was tough. I cried myself to sleep when I came from lunch with him. BUT I feel like it was a good release. He handled it well.

Kema: Yeah sometimes it's good to release. I know you don't indulge in conversation about your angel baby. But I think it's healthy especially with her father. You two are connected forever in that way. I'm sure he was dealing with some unresolved stuff about it as well.

Joye: Yeah, he was. He couldn't believe it had been 15 years.

Ro: Shit I can't believe it either. Wow. Time.

Joye: We talked about the boy too?

Ro: The boy? huh?

Kema: Oh SHIT! For realzzzzzzzzzzzzzz?

Ro: oh!!!! THE boy. Ezekiel???? Damnnnnn. Journee and Zeke in the same day? Y'all doing fo' much. But I love it.

Joye: I'm drained.

Joye: We're having dinner tonight.

Ro: Where? I'm coming too.

Joye: oh god

Kema: Do not tell her. Her ass will show up.

Joye: I already know.

Ro: No. I will wait until y'all get things completely worked out before I start crashing y'all dates. I have some respecK.

Ro: Hey

Ro: How do you feel about him? Do you think y'all can get back together?

Kema: Well, I'm feeling great about it. 🌝

Ro: Not you weirdo!

Joye: I think we're going to be okay. Baby steps though...

Ro: Asè

Kema: Yaaaasssssssss I'm happy for you.

Ro: Umm, on a ratchet note. Has anyone spoken to Mallia?

Kema: Uhhhh, NOPE!

Joye: No. I was thinking about calling her, but I just can't deal right now.

Ro: Do not call her. What about Jordin?

Kema: It's still a NOPE for me dawg. 👎

Ro: Same. Well she texted me asking how everyone was doing but I ignored her.

Joye: Maybe she should just reach out to everyone herself and ask? Just an idea.

Kema: She don't have to call me. I'm skkkkkkkkraight. lol

Joye: Abe sent me a text. It said he understands if I don't want to talk but he'd like an opportunity to explain.

Ro: Ninja, please.

Joye: I left his ass on read. I don't have time for him.

Ro: Please stay focused on yourself and Ferst, if he's serious. Don't let these tired ass distractions trip you up. And, please know that when I say I love Ferst and I miss him and call him our husband that I am just expressing how amazing I think you two are together. I would never pull a Mallia on you. I want you to be happy!

Joye: Oh, I'm not. And, boo, I know. He loves you too. Smh.

Joye: I gotta get my life together. I told Ferst I wanted to stay in so I should probably get some dinner going. I'll talk to you silly hoes later. Love y'all.

Kema: <3

Ro: 143 (old school on ya asses) Xoxo

Joye decided against cooking. She was lazy and not in the mood to slave over the stove.

She called Ferst and asked him to grab takeout for dinner. She said he could choose anything he wanted and swore she would not be too picky. He told her he was already two steps ahead of the game and had placed a to-go order for an 8 o'clock pick up and would arrive by 8:30 p.m.

It was an official date.

Joye and Ferst were both secretly hoping the night would turn into an adult sleepover, but neither of them were ready to admit it to each other. So while Joye prepared her home for her date with Ferst, she also prepared her body by shaving and making sure she smelled good everywhere. And, Ferst made a stop at the CVS downstairs from her apartment building and bought himself a box of condoms. He smirked at the thought of Joye denying his offer to try and knock her up.

Joye was battling with her own girlish wonders of what the night might bring. She felt like a teenager about to sneak out of the house to be with her crush. After only two days she had started to let her guard down. And, with a solid physical attraction, she wasn't so sure she wouldn't want more than dinner.

The battle of the outfits began. She didn't know if she wanted to be sexy, casual, or elegant. She got fed up as time quickly began running out and chose what she always puts on when she wants to feel sexy yet dressed down: a two-piece fitness get up with leggings and a long-sleeved crop top. She decided to let her natural hair flow and just be a curly chick that night.

She made a last-minute check of the house to make sure everything was presentable for her guest. She inspected the toilets, made sure there was tissue on the roll in the bathroom, and soap in the dispenser. She laid out fresh hand towels and emptied the trash. She opened a closet and reached up on the shelf and grabbed Jenga and a box of UNO cards.

Moments later her phone rang. It was her concierge requesting permission to send Ferst upstairs.

"Good Evening, Ms. Allyn. This is your concierge, Ramon. I have Mr. Upton here to see you."

"Hi, Ramon. Send him up. Thanks!" Joye smiled. She went and rinsed with mouthwash, checked her eyes, hair, and sniffed her armpits. She walked to the kitchen, grabbed a bottle of honey, and rubbed a drop of it onto her lips before opening the door. Before Ferst could even say hello she kissed him directly on the mouth. It was a nice long kiss.

Ferst was pretty shocked that Joye did that. "Somebody is happy to see me." Joye was usually more subtle and slow to burn but over the years she had gotten more experienced and in touch with her sensual side.

"You taste delicious." Ferst licked his lips to pull the rest of her sweetness onto him.

"I am happy to see you." She reached for the bags in his hand. "But I'm mo' happy to see what's in the bag. What's for dinner?" She said playfully.

"Calm down. Calm down. Can I get in the door good before you start attacking me? " Ferst took his shoes off, sat the bags onto the kitchen island, and washed his hands. Joye watched him unpack the to-go food containers like he was performing at a male revue or something.

"Excuse me? You are making me uncomfortable, woman!" He joked with her.

"Whatever. Cut it out. You better be lucky someone likes looking at you?"

"Someone? Or you?"

Joye evaded the question. She stepped back and looked him up and down to really check him out.

"So this what you wear to a date? Basketball shorts and a hoodie? You look hideous."

"I look sexy. What you talmbout? You said you ain't wanna go nowhere." Ferst opened his arms and took a seat at the kitchen island. "I got a suit in the car. You want me to put that on?"

"No, Negro."

Joye dished the food onto a plate for Ferst. He doesn't drink alcohol, so she served him bottled water and a pomegranate Izze, then poured herself a glass of Intercepts Red Blend. She jumped on her countertop and ate from the foam containers.

"Oh, you straight project. You went from classy to ashy in less than 60 seconds!" But that wasn't it. Joye was completely free.

"Whatever! I have never, ever, ever, ever lived in the projects. That's your territory, Boo."

"So you baggin' on my childhood? I see how you do me." Ferst pretended to whine, "Imma tell my mama."

"She ain't gon' do nothing but agree with me. Everybody knows I'm her favorite ex."

"That's true. You know? She asks about you all the time. Everybody does."

"Well, hopefully, you say nice things about me."

"Of course. There's nothing not nice about you. Other than you dragging your knuckles over that counter and eating like a Neanderthal, you're kinda cute." Joye and Ferst went back and forth joning on each other through dinner. Talking about old times and enjoying each other's company. They laughed so hard until their stomachs and faces hurt.

Joye started clearing the mess they'd made of the food and drink. They made their way to the living room where she had Jenga and a deck of UNO cards sitting on the table.

"Oh! This is what you want?" Ferst cracked his knuckles and stretched like he was preparing to enter a real fight. Joye and Ferst have always had a healthy level of competition between them. But she was terrible. She wanted to compete in spaces where she actually sucked. Jenga wasn't her strong suit, and she definitely couldn't beat him at UNO.

Joye started hip-hopping around the living room like she was in a Run DMC video from the 80s.

"Are you ready to get this beat down?" Joye sang out to the melody of the legendary "Let's Get Ready to Rumble" phrase.

Ferst accepted the challenge. "Which game do you want to lose first?"

"You're the visitor. It's your call, Homie."

"You have clearly lost your mind. I'm a winner at life, Baby! Ain't no way in hell you're about to beat me at a card game. Let's go."

"So, UNO it is. You wanna put some money on this?"

"I accept CashApp."

There was a lot of shit-talking during this game. It was like watching Shaq and Kobe. Ferst was Kobe, of course. Joye was just out there clowning making a fool of herself trying to bully him off the table. She was yelling and singing 'Where dem dollars at?' every time she made a winning play. She was really out of control, but she was having such a good time. So was Ferst. Then she took it there; she took the game straight to cheater's land.

"Skip you!

"Reverse back to me!

"Draw four!

"Draw four more!

"Skip yo ass again!

"Draw two more!

"UNO. OUT!"

Joye stood up and did a victory lap and dance. She posed like the Heisman Trophy a few times all while yelling "Boom!"

She had the nerve to dance the little Lebron James victory dance. She was amped up.

"Ahhh hell no! Yo' ass cheating like a mug!"

Joye sat down on the floor and stacked the UNO cards. "Well, dear. What's that you said about being a winner at life? What had happened?" Joye said sarcastically.

"You cheated, that's what had happened."

"Aww. Don't look so sad. I'll let you win next time. Okay?"

Ferst shook his head, "Unbelievable."

There were a few moments of silence. Joye brought more bottled water and snacks to the living room. She pulled out a couple of throw blankets and burrowed into the couch.

"A movie?" She motioned to Ferst to join her on the couch. He wanted to get closer to her and feel the heat from her body, smell her hair, and kiss her lips again. Ferst had sense enough to position himself behind her and allow her to relax into his chest. He was a little concerned at how long he could last in that position before his manhood would rise and he started stabbing her in the back.

Joye fiddled around with the remote control for a second then decided on *The Lost Boys.*

Then she turned her head to look Ferst in his eyes and said, "I noticed you never even looked at your phone tonight? Thank you."

"You're welcome."

"I promise not to make my little observation an expectation, but I did want you to know that I appreciate you for doing that."

Fest was surprised to get that compliment from Joye. There was a time when she only acknowledged the bad that he did, so he was excited to witness her be all grown up.

"Ah, thank you for noticing my effort. It was deliberate. And, thank you for the expectation thing. You know how life gets? I definitely don't want to make promises I can't keep but I want to work on listening to your needs and doing my best to honor them."

"Sweet. I like that."

It was already 11:30 p.m. The runtime on the movie was an hour and thirty-seven minutes. Ferst still wasn't sure if he had an invitation to spend the night—even though it seemed like he did. He eventually stopped thinking about all of that and tried to enjoy the movie.

Ferst spent more time looking at Joye and listening to her heartbeat and breaths than watching the movie. He was happy she let him back in and held on to her with all his might. He hadn't done that in fifteen years. Her silence was loud, her energy was deafening. Joye needed him and Ferst needed her.

They never finished that movie. Joye fell asleep twenty minutes in and when she woke up decided she wanted to get into her bed. She wiped her eyes and said, "You coming?" Ferst's eyes widened and he followed her to her bedroom. He was thinking that this would be a perfect ending to a perfect night if they jumped on each other and had wild, passionate sex, but that did not happen. She didn't deny him, and he knew that he had full access to her at that moment. But he sensed that sex was not what she needed. She didn't make a major move and he didn't take any. Her sweet honey kiss was going to have to be enough to tide him over for the night.

Ferst stripped to his boxers and she laid on his chest. He wrapped his arms around her waist, kissed her on her forehead, and whispered, "Good night."

She whispered back, "Thank you."

☙

Family Ferst

It would be six months later before Joye and Melanie would take the trip to see their mother. That reminder Joye set in her phone had been moved 10 times. Joye was no fool. Even though time passed her mother would knock her out if she forgot.

"Joye! Do not make us late, asshole!"

Melanie was hollering from the garage while she loaded the trunk of Joye's car. Joye had forgotten something inside her apartment and ran back to get it. They were headed to see their mom for a couple of days. Melanie was even more anal retentive than Joye was. Talk about being a planner. Melanie would schedule trips down to the minute. She would literally hand her travel buddies a printed out itinerary that was formatted like a run of show.

"Okay, I am 'ret ta go'! And, I heard you call me an asshole, asshole." Joye and Melanie fake windmilled each other.

"Let's go sistah, sistah!" Joye was such a TV nerd. That was her Mowry sisters' sitcom theme song impression.

"You gotta be smoking crack." They loaded the car and pulled off.

"No, baby sis. I am high off life. Who needs crack? Crack is cheap and—"

They both said in unison, "Crack is wack!" They listened to music and danced in the car on the way to the airport.

"Hey, Ma asked me to remind her to remember to tell us something when we got there. So I am reminding you to remind me to remind her to remember what she wants to tell us."

"Girl stop it. Both are y'all are retarded."

"Don't shoot the messenger. I'm just telling you what your mama said."

"Hey, how is therapy going?"

"It's good. Dr. Ellis is the truth. I mean, I do most of the work, but she helps me get there. You know? Like your husband and most of the sorry, ugly teeny wiener boyfriends you've had?"

"You know I can't stand you, right?" Melanie kept her cool and smiled a little at Joye's dig. "Have you spoken to Mallia?"

"No. Not yet. I really want her to call me. But we'll see. Maybe I need to let them get married and then go from there. I'm not trippin' though."

"Well, that's mature." Melanie was hesitant to bring it up but could no longer hold it in, "I know this is old news but it was weird seeing her and Jordin at that fiasco of an engagement party of yours! Why would he invite them?"

Joye shook her head. "Because he's stupid. I dunno. Maybe he forgot that we had a little issue."

"Anyway, we don't care about him." Melanie moved right into the question she really wanted to ask, "How are you and Mr. Ferst?"

Joye's face lit up. "We're good. Nothing major is going on right now. Just getting reacquainted and enjoying our time together. The last 6 months have been pretty awesome, actually."

Melanie looked at Joye and nodded her head in agreement very slowly. "He is a good guy. I approve of him. Eee-ven though you guys have trauma ties."

"Melanie, stop. You are not a counselor. Your husband is.

Never forget." Joye was a little annoyed with her sister commenting on her love life from what seemed like a pedestal.

"I'm not trying to be a counselor. I'm trying to say that I am proud of the way you two have been able to remain friends over the years and now work through your heartaches. It's admirable. I'm not sure that I would be able to do it. I'm rooting for you guys."

"Aww. That's so sweet. Thank you. I think we'll be fine. I am just taking my time and trying to stay out of my head. Stop creating relationships based on what I want them to be as opposed to what they really are."

"Well, good because I'm ready for a wedding."

They arrived at the airport parking garage and began unloading their bags.

"Oh, God! I'm sure that won't be happening anytime soon so relax."

"What do you think mom has to tell us?"

"Black Neeguh! I have no idea. Why are you asking me questions like I know? I don't know! You will find out when I find out. Oh my God! It's like we're 5-years-old again."

Joye mocked Melanie by reciting a bunch of silly questions that a toddler would ask. They both cracked up laughing as they walked into the airport.

સ

Joye and Melanie were expecting their mom to have prepared a huge home-cooked meal for them when they arrived. Instead, when they called her to let her know they had landed, she told them to stop at the Giordano's on Cicero and pick up the deep dish cheese and spinach pizza she ordered for them.

The girls looked at each other and simultaneously said, "She trippin'!"

Mrs. Allyn was as beautiful as ever when she opened the door to greet her girls.

"Hey, gorgeous," Joye said after giving her mom a big kiss.

Melanie hugged her mom, "Hi, Mommy."

Mrs. Allyn was all smiles, "Hey! Hey! Y'all made it!"

Once the girls got settled in they sat down at the dining room table for dinner. Dinner quickly turned into a cuddle session on the big comfy couch with Mrs. Allyn's fluffy throw blankets. They decided to watch some episodes of "*Criminal Minds*" on Netflix.

Melanie blurted out, "Oh, gross! Y'all are gonna be having nightmares tonight from watching this!"

"What language are you speaking, honey?" Mrs. Allyn was more horrified by Melanie's poor grammar than the gruesome scenes from the television show.

Joye's phone rang. Surprisingly, it was Mallia, and when she picked up, Abe was also on the line. Mrs. Allyn and Melanie listened intensely for a moment, then signaled for Joye to put the call on speakerphone after realizing who was on the other end of the line.

"I'm glad you both decided to call me, but I think if this had happened before you guys got too serious it wouldn't even be a thing between us, ya know?" Joye explained.

Mallia had an attitude. "Well, our relationship has nothing to do with you, Joye! Why would we be thinking about you when we're in the process of building our life together?"

"Umm, because I was supposed to be your friend and Abe

was my boyfriend at one time. Hello?" Joye was confused that Mallia was having such a hard time understanding.

Abe spoke up, "You're right, Joye. We should have said something."

Mallia screamed in the background, "Why are you agreeing with her?!"

"Because I'm right." Joye laughed. "Listen, my position isn't going to change about this. But y'all be happy together. I wish you both well. I really do."

"Oh, please! Joye, you do not wish us well. You have always been jealous of any woman that had a man because you don't know how to keep one. I heard about your latest break up with Bryce. Some engagement, huh?"

Mrs. Allyn and Melanie's mouths were wide opened. They could not believe she said that.

Joye was hurt but not surprised that Mallia was so angry with her. "Really, Mallia? This is how you feel?"

"Yes. All you care about is your career. Making money and living some lifestyle that no man can ever live up to. Why do you think Abe left your controlling ass?"

"Left? Girl stop it. If you believe that shit you are dumber than you sound right now." Joye looked over to her mother and mouthed, "Sorry, Ma."

The lies and disrespect Mallia spewed at Joye over her decision to love Abe was childish to say the least. Joye only asked for an apology from them for not making her aware earlier. They didn't agree with her point of view and they didn't want to concede; they just wanted to explain themselves.

Mrs. Allyn and Melanie tried to whisper pointers to help Joye with that conversation, but nothing really worked. Mallia was set on being rude and Abe was just following along with whatever Mallia said once she shut him down.

Joye had made peace with her breakup with Abe a long time ago, but Mallia was a new wound and she was going to need a little time to get some understanding.

The girls burrowed themselves back onto the couch each taking one of their mom's shoulders, and continued watching TV.

"That child was never your friend. Good riddance," Mrs. Allyn said softly before kissing Joye on the top of her head.

ॐ

Joye, Melanie, and their mom spent the next few mornings cooking breakfast together, going on morning walks, and eating tubs of ice cream while watching old movies.

Joye had been reminding her mom about the conversation they needed to have, and on their last night with her, Mrs. Allyn sat the girls down for a serious talk.

"You know your father loved you both with his whole heart. When you were younger I would get jealous sometimes because you two had him wrapped around your little fingers and I couldn't get him to give me five measly uninterrupted minutes!"

The girls smiled. They were wondering where this conversation was going to go. Mrs. Allyn continued, "Most men want at least one son but not your father," She reflected. "He was a good man, not a perfect man. Do you understand the difference?"

Joye's spidey senses were raised, "Mom, what are you trying to tell us?"

"Yeah, Ma, what's going on?" Melanie asked.

Mrs. Allyn explained that about ten years ago their father confided to her about a relationship he had around the same time they met. There was a daughter born of that relationship. For years, Mr. Allyn had been secretly trying to find the little girl he desperately wanted to bring his family together. Mrs. Allyn told the girls that she was beyond upset that their father kept such a huge secret, but she eventually got involved in the search. Unfortunately, nothing concrete ever surfaced until about two years ago.

"That's why we never mentioned it to you girls. We wanted to be sure." Mrs. Allyn said.

Right before Mr. Allyn became extremely ill, he received a letter from a young lady saying she believed she was his daughter. "We were in the midst of making arrangements to meet and conduct a DNA test, but we never got around it." Mrs. Allyn said. "After your father passed, I still wanted to find out the truth."

Melanie and Joye were in complete shock.

Mrs. Allyn grabbed an envelope and handed the letter to Melanie and the pictures to Joye. Mrs. Allyn was 100% certain that this would cause a ripple in the family, but she also believed that her girls were forgiving and would be able to see beyond the hurt and embrace their sister regardless of the circumstances. But that is not what happened.

Joye immediately jumped up screaming, "No. No way. This isn't true, Ma." Joye kept shaking her head.

Melanie grabbed the picture from Joye's hand and covered her mouth in disbelief. "Ma! That's Aubrii, Ezekiel's mom!"

"Who!?"

Mrs. Allyn never would have made the connection to Joye and Ferst because she was never privy to the details of Joye's love life. Joye always kept hush about things that would arm her parents with ammunition to hate people she once loved. Of course, they knew Ferst had a son, but that's all they knew. When the girls saw the pictures and the name on the letter of this long, lost daughter, Joye had no choice but to fill her mom in on the details surrounding exactly who Aubrii was.

It was a tough night. For obvious reasons, Joye headed home immediately.

ॐ

Two days had passed since Joye returned home, and she was at the gym trying to work off some steam.

Melanie stayed through her original return date, but they were equally emotional wrecks. Melanie relied on her husband's expertise and counsel incessantly over the last 72 hours. Joye really didn't know what to do so she worked out, she vented to her friends and she had an emergency session with Dr. Ellis.

Joye was avoiding Ferst's calls and texts, and he had no idea why. He stopped by her apartment a few times, but she requested that her concierge deny him access. "I'm sorry Mr. Upton, Miss Allyn is unavailable."

"You didn't even call her!?" Ferst noted.

"I'm sorry, Mr. Upton," the Concierge said.

Joye knew he was concerned about her, but she was so angry she didn't want to talk to or see him. Maybe ever again.

Ro texted Joye.

Ro: Hey babe, Ferst hit me up on IG. He's worried about you? What do you want me to tell him?

Joye: Nothing. I'm headed to his house now. I'm going to talk to him.

Ro: Okay, babe. Let me know if you need me.

Joye was standing on the front porch of Ferst's house. He barely put the car in park when he saw Joye and jumped out. As he hurried over to her he asked, "Baby. What's going on? What's wrong? Are you okay? I've been calling and texting. What's going on?"

Joye didn't open her mouth. Ferst opened his front door and tried to convince her to take a few breaths and talk to him. But she was spilling over with rage.

Joye took her post in the living room.

"Please tell me what's going on?" Ferst begged her.

In an emotional rant, she unveiled the unimaginable news she learned about Aubrii. Ferst's response was the same as everyone else's: disbelief.

"Did you know?!" She screamed.

Ferst screamed right back. "How could I fucking know?"

"Answer the question, Ferst!"

Joye thought they were finally in the clear zone. She never could have imagined that they'd be fighting again about the very thing that broke them up fifteen years ago.

"No. Oh, God. Babe, No! I-I didn't know," Ferst said trying to gain his composure.

Joye was also trying to make sense of the new reality. She wanted to blame someone.

"That woman looks just like me! You didn't think to ask questions? You should have asked questions. You should have paid closer attention. You should ha—"

"Do you hear yourself? I am not perfect! And, apparently, your father wasn't either. You walk around here like you have never fucked up. Well you have and you do, okay? Yes, Joye fucks up too! The difference between me and you is I don't complain about what you do, don't do or could have and should have done all the damn time."

"Well, that's your problem. Maybe if you talked to me and told me what was going on or bothering you about me I could fix it," Joye argued.

Ferst tried to gain control, "That's just it. You don't need to fix everything. Even this. This is not something we can fix. It just is." Ferst wiped his hand across his face in frustration.

"Come here. Please listen to me. You have got to know that I'm a lot of things, but I am not *that*. I have never sought anybody out to purposely hurt you. I barely knew that woman. And, a-and I know it's fucked up that I made a kid with a stranger in the midst of trying to love you. I don't have an excuse for that. But your sister? Your fucking sister? Come on man. There's no way I did that shit on purpose! How would I know? Huh? How would I know?!" Ferst pleaded. He needed Joye to believe and understand him.

Joye walked out.

She was done.

Ferst watched Joye drive down that long ass driveway. She felt further away from him than she had ever felt. Neither of them had an answer; no tricks up their sleeves, no impassioned speeches, no grand gestures to repair this.

Joye wanted to cry but she was vexed. She kept mumbling, "Fucking liar!"

Ferst closed his front door and repeated over and over again while holding his head in frustration, "Aubrii is Joye's sister? What the fuck?"

※

The next day Joye was sprawled out on Dr. Ellis' couch. She was a total mess. She wore oversized sweatpants, a t-shirt, a jean jacket, and a baseball cap. She looked like she had been grocery shopping or moving all day, but she had done neither. Joye just wanted to look how she felt--torn up.

After she told Dr. Ellis of the tumultuous trip to Chicago the doctor was desperate to help Joye move through the mess her father made and move through it quickly.

"How would Ferst have known that the woman he cheated on you with all the way in California was your half-sister? If he didn't know that a half-sister even existed and you didn't know you had a half-sister, how could knowing be his responsibility?" Dr. Ellis tried to bring some logic into Joye's session.

"It wouldn't."

"And, your sister? She also had no idea? As a matter of fact, she still doesn't know. Is that correct?"

"As far as I know."

"So in his death, your father has left quite a mess for you and your family to clean up. I am sorry about that. But this doesn't have to be a death sentence, Joye. Just because you feel betrayed and hurt doesn't mean that you have to live in that feeling. Do you understand? There are some opportunities for forgiveness and healing here. I do not recommend setting fire to everyone and everything in your path just because you got burned. Does that make sense?

"This is not his fault. It's not your fault. It's not Aubrii's fault. It's not even your father's fault. Let's not focus on blame here. I want you to begin to focus on what your family needs and how to move forward, if you so choose, with all parties involved. This is a lot for everyone to handle."

Joye wasn't prepared to hear and deal with this part of life. Never in a million years did she imagine that the reminder she had set aside in her phone six months ago was such a sinister secret and downright betrayal of her trust. The pain caused by her father's infidelity and the uncovering of the truths surrounding it was a hard horse pill to swallow

Ferst Come, Ferst Serve

Joye stopped by Melanie's house for one of her usual Saturday pop-ins. Her niece Sara was sure to give her all the smiles she needed.

Kyle opened the door for Joye, "Good morning, sister-in-law. How are you doing?"

"I'm hanging in here brother-in-law. How are you? You sick? You look terrible" Joye's blunt mouth was unaffected by her heartbreak.

"You're such an asshole. I'm not sick. You know I've been working on my doctorate degree. I'm exhausted."

"Word? I did not know. That's awesome. Congrats."

"Yeah. Mel is giving Sara a bath," Kyle's eyes were closed as he spoke and he was rubbing his head. "That kid has been acting like the Tasmanian Devil all week."

Joye laughed. "Her momma is the Tasmanian Devil. Kid gets it honestly."

Joye trotted up the stairs to the bathroom and found her niece and sister exactly where Kyle said they would be.

"Hey, babe." Joye kissed Melanie on the cheek and waved to Sara who was covered in bubbles. "What is happening here?"

"She is driving me crazy. Between her terrible threes, her father's stress, and my bad attitude we are in a rut over here at the Turner residence."

"Girl, have you guys been able to get out and have some fun?"

Melanie quipped, "What's that?"

"You know you can drop her to me any time? You can also visit. You can also bring her when you visit," Joye said. "You can pack a bag and just come by—."

"I get it. I know. I will. Soon."

"You need to." Joye never understood why her sister didn't hang out with her unless they were traveling or Joye was stopping by her place. She assumed it was part of the married life. No time for outsiders. "Have you talked to Ma?"

"Yes. She is driving me crazy too. You need to call her and answer all of her questions."

"Uhhh, nope. She needs to sort out her husband's affairs. Pun intended. I'll call her when I sort out mine."

"You're such an asshole"

"You know your husband said those exact words to me downstairs. Is that how y'all refer to me in this house? Let me find out. Haters."

Well, since you haven't spoken to your mammy, let me fill you in. She doesn't think—hold on. Sara stop splashing the water!" Melanie was in the midst of losing her shit. She was on edge unlike Joye had ever seen her before.

"Hey. Go. Let me finish her bath. I'll bring her down when she's clean and dressed. Cool?"

"Thanks. I need to eat something. My head is pounding."

Melanie stood up and hugged Joye. It was the kind of hug that said I need this more than you.

"I got you!"

Joye spent a good hour with Sara. She dressed her and played with stuffed animals and dolls. She pulled out electronic toys that were so annoying that after five minutes she took all the batteries out and pretended they were broken. It was close to noon, which was usually naptime for Sara, so she tried to wear her down. She laid in the bed with Sara and told her to grab her favorite book so they could read and fall asleep into dreamland. Sara grabbed a family favorite, *Goodnight, Moon*. Sara was sleepy, so by the time Joye read the last few words of the book her niece was out for the count.

Just then Melanie appeared in the doorway.

She was overwhelmed with emotion as she saw Joye lifting herself from Sara's bed gently. Joye bent down and kissed her niece on the forehead. When she turned around Melanie was looking at her with tears in her eyes and began talking and crying at the same time. "You would have been a great mother, Joye. I am so sorry that this is happening to you and to our family. This shit is so unfair."

"Aww. Don't make me cry! Stop it. It's okay. Let's not wake her up. Come on."

Joye put her arms around her sister and they walked into the guest bedroom. Melanie was very upset.

"Hey? I'm okay. I promise."

"I'm not. So much going on around here. And your mother! She is Inspector Gadget 24/7. It's annoying. How is she not pissed off?"

"She's had more than enough time to be pissed off. She means well. She just wants to get to the bottom of it."

"She's definitely going to do that. So, I was telling you earlier before I had a mental breakdown that she has been talking to Aubrii. And, she isn't 100% sure that the girl is our father's daughter. But she is trying to figure out how to schedule DNA tests and all of that stuff."

"Oh, God. The woman has gone mad!" Joye said in an English accent.

"Right! I told her I wasn't going to participate in any of it. So, I'm not sure how she's going about all of it. Anyway, mom has also been talking to Ezekiel like every single day. So you can deal with that. How are you and Ferst?"

Joye made a face." Uhhh. We are, no, I am not good. I ignored him for a few days and then popped at his front door and screamed at him like a crazy woman. He has been checking in, but I have been an asshole." Immediately realizing what she called herself she said, "See? It *is* this house. This house forces you to call me an asshole."

Melanie nodded in agreement. "It's a smart house, ya know? "Seriously, what do you think you are going to do?"

Shaking her head Joye acknowledged that she did not know what she was going to do.

"What do you want to do?" Melanie wanted to know so she could properly support her sister.

"I don't really know."

"Yes, you do! Stop answering with what you think other people want to hear or will accept! What do YOU want to do?" Melanie demanded.

"I want us to be okay. I want us to move through it if that's possible."

"Without excusing the original sin, Sis, he didn't do this on purpose. You can't let him do dad's bid."

"You're right. I know."

"And, as your sister, I can say this. Fuck that bitch! We don't know her. She may not even be our sister. And, if she is, so what! We still may never get to know her as a sister. So, don't let someone who already claims stake in your man's life dictate how you move forward with him. I know it sounds weird and it's not how any of us would imagine it, but damn, that man loves yo' dirty ass drawls. And I've seen your drawls." Joye and Melanie laughed and hugged each other.

"Shut up! Oh my goodness what has gotten into you? Let's go downstairs." Joyed called out, "Kyle! Do you carry any alcoholic beverages in this house? Your wife needs a bottle of something, anything, STAT!"

"Shhh! You are going to wake up Sara you asshole!"

‪

Ferst Love

For five more months the family would be in an almost silent war.

Melanie was juggling her life with Kyle's higher learning endeavors, Sara's terrible fours now, and the fallout of Mr. Allyn's little secret.

Kyle was doing the same, only he was losing his ever-loving mind trying to be a full-time dad, therapist, husband, and student. No extracurricular activities for him made him a dull boy, and he was already a geek.

Mrs. Allyn was in full Maury Povich mode and working nonstop to field information from Aubrii and Ezekiel and tie up her deceased husband's loose strings as it related to his two daughters and a possible. She was also trying to keep her relationship with her daughters on the up and up, and they weren't always as interested in the lovechild debauchery that she had consumed herself with.

Kema and Ro were going about their normal lives working, dating, and remaining good and loyal friends. They both had started dating seriously and were being pulled in multiple directions. They were tuned in and especially concerned with Joye when things got rough. This silent war was one that no one knew how or when it would end, but these two soldiers stayed suited up and prepared to battle at a minutes' notice.

Jordin removed herself from the circle but kept in touch. She was more of a friend to Mallia, so it made sense that she'd pull away even further after Mallia and Joye severed ties.

Mallia and Abe eloped. They couldn't wait to get married and have little disloyal babies together. Mallia moved away to be with Abe when he got a new job in Florida, and no one missed them.

Ferst was treading lightly and keeping his nose clean and trying to be responsible with work, his son, and Joye.

Aubrii was being Aubrii. She didn't change her position. She didn't want anything to do with Joye's family or Ferst. She was actually beginning to find joy in the possibility of being more of a thorn for Joye and Ferst.

Despite the crazy news, Joye and Ferst were getting closer to normal quicker than expected. She was closing new clients at rapid speed, and Ferst was busy as ever. Sometimes their projects aligned in the same location, allowing them to spend some time together when on the road. Sometimes Ro and Kema would work as consultants on some of Joye's projects and get to travel with her so they were having a ball getting reacquainted with Ferst and Joye as a couple.

Joye was still rejecting Ferst's offer to move into his big mansion. She said she was done rushing things and was satisfied with life as it was, for now.

Joye and Ferst used the words "for now" often because they wanted to be flexible and thoughtful about building their life together. They had made a new commitment to each other. With her 'assholiness' and his bullheadedness, they'd probably have to recommit to each other over and over and over again. Many of their ideas were non-traditional. They were a million miles away from a normal relationship and they had been fighting their way to and through healthy for a long, long time. Joye and Ferst were in agreement that they wanted their relationship to work, forever. Whatever it meant to keep them together, they were down for the fight as long as it was together.

Occasionally Joye would schedule a meeting with Ferst to discuss how they were coming along and what they needed to do, if anything, to be a better version of themselves.

One time she ended their talk by singing "Everwanting: To Want You to Want" by Maxwell and Joye could not sing.

She started talking off-topic and really out of nowhere in the middle of singing her song. "You know what I'm really ever wanting from you, Babe?"

"Huh?" Ferst was trying to finish his last set of sit-ups before he jumped in bed.

"I want reparations." Joye was dead serious.

"Reparations? Reparations for what!?" Ferst stopped mid-sit up.

Joye was throwing the 700 pillows she bought for his bed on the floor. "For the struggle love course you've been steering us onto."

"Aww, damn. So I'm the driver?"

"I'm just saying..."

"Alright. Cool. Forty ounces and a meal coming right up!" If they could find humor in it, they knew they would be okay.

"So tomorrow's a big day?" Ferst asked.

"It really is."

"How are you feeling?" He shrugged.

"Meh. I think what I am feeling is a mixture of nerves and being pissed." It was a big day for both of them.

Joye asked Ferst, "How are *you* feeling?

They were a day away from making the big trip to end, or continue, the silent war. Mrs. Allyn had arranged for Joye and Melanie to travel to Oakland to meet Aubrii and get DNA tests. Melanie declined. She wanted no parts of helping provide proof that her father had a child outside of his marriage to her mother. Joye saw this as an opportunity to clear the air and find out the truth. It was also an opportunity for Joye to be introduced to Aubrii and Zeke under new circumstances. Everyone was hoping for a smooth meeting.

ॐ

First Borns

Joye, Mrs. Allyn, and Ferst landed in San Francisco. None of them had checked luggage, so they made a dash for the Air Train and headed to the rental car facility. Everyone was unusually quiet; however, it was understandable. There was a lot to be discovered.

Joye's mother had never been to the West Coast, so she was dropping hints about sightseeing.

"Mom? I think Joye needs to sleep. She doesn't look so good," Ferst said.

Joye glared at Ferst and rolled her eyes. "Tell her the truth. You don't want to do it." Joye ratted on Ferst.

"Daaaaamn. You are supposed to have my back?"

"And you're supposed to have mine." Joye snapped back.

"I can't argue about that."

Mrs. Allyn didn't want to make them do anything they didn't want to do so she said, "It's fine you guys. Don't get all bent out of shape because of me. We could all use some rest."

Joye said, "We're not bent out of shape, Mom," but her tone suggested otherwise.

Ferst took them to the hotel and they all checked in. He asked for dining recommendations at the front desk, but Joye wanted to get under the bed, literally.

Joye walked into the room and immediately began to undress. She stripped down to her bra and panties and got straight into the bed.

Joye was struggling with the whole purpose of the trip. Ferst asked her if she wanted to talk.

"No, Baby. I just want to rest."

Tomorrow would arrive very quickly. Ferst, Joye, and Mrs. Allyn met in the lobby for breakfast. Joye had to have her morning cup of coffee. Her mother ordered tea, a croissant, and scrambled eggs, and Ferst ordered water for his protein powder.

"I have to be at the lab at 11. Maybe we can knock out some sightseeing for Ma?" Joye suggested.

"Okay. And lunch with Zeke and his mom?" Ferst asked, but the jury was split.

Mrs. Allyn said, "Yes."

Joye followed with a hard, "No."

"No?" Ferst confirmed.

Joye was firm, "No. I don't want to sit and eat with her before we have our results. I will have lunch with Ezekiel, but not her. Not right now."

Because Aubrii was the mother of Ferst's son Joye knew they were going to have to communicate and interact in some way, at some point, but today was not the day. Joye thought Ferst was being inconsiderate.

"Baby, you know we won't receive the results for at least 4 days?"

Joye quickly answered, "Yep."

"Okay. I will grab Ezekiel for lunch after you take your test. And—," Ferst stopped himself mid-thought "Yeah. That's what we'll do."

They all agreed to try to enjoy themselves, but no one was having a good time. They decided to pick up Zeke before Joye's appointment since they had to pass by his house to get to the lab. It had been a very long time since Joye had seen him and Mrs. Allyn had never met him at all. Ferst hadn't seen Zeke in a while, but that was the norm.

Aubrii made sure to step out on her porch when they picked up Zeke. She wanted to be seen.

Ezekiel had a big smile on his face. His hair was longer, and he had a scratch under his eye. He was a good looking kid. Long and lean with broad shoulders. He was the perfect mixture of his mom and dad.

"What's up, Dad?" Ezekiel dapped his father.

"Boy, give me a hug. And what's up with that base in your voice?"

Ezekiel continued to smile as he let his father rough him up a little bit and give a few man hugs.

Joye noticed Aubrii. She no longer looked like the photo she had seen at her mother's house. The image showed a strong resemblance to Joye but that was less prevalent today. Aubrii was a pretty woman, especially fifteen years ago. She was a little taller, a little darker in complexion, with more prominent features than Joye. But depending on the angle and the lighting Ferst could see what Joye meant when she said Aubrii looked just like her, especially fifteen years ago.

Ferst walked his son over towards the car, "Zeke, I have a few people I want you to meet."

"Yeah. I know. Ma told me."

"Well, I'll tell the real version later. Be nice."

"I'm always nice. What you talkin' about man?" Ezekiel pretended to swing a baseball bat and pointed to signal a home run.

"Get in the car," Ferst said, then introduced Zeke to Joye and her mother.

They all shared small talk before stopping at the lab. The appointment was supposed to be 30 minutes because it was a noninvasive procedure. Joye simply went in and got swabbed, but it took about an hour and a half. Joye completed the paperwork and an intake interview. The nurse explained the process and eventually Joye was done.

Joye walked into the lobby where everyone was waiting and said, "Alright kids. Let's go eat!" But she was disturbed to see Aubrii there. Aubrii's appointment was at 12 o'clock.

Ferst stood up and nervously greeted Joye. "Hey, Baby. How'd it go?"

"It was too long but fine."

"Hey, umm, this is Ezekiel's mom, Aubrii. Aubrii, this is Joye."

Aubrii was eager to offer a handshake. "Hi. Nice to meet you."

Joye nodded her head in acknowledgment of her.

"I guess we'll be finding out if we are sisters soon enough, huh?" Aubrii was way too friendly and in your face at this particular time for Joye's taste.

Joye responded with a very fake smile and another head nod. She turned to Ferst and said, "We're going to be late to our next appointment. We should get outta here." Joye turned back to Aubrii. "Nice meeting you. Ezekiel is amazing."

Ferst agreed, "Right. Come on, son. You're with us today."

Aubrii corrected Ferst. "Actually, he's with me today. Change of plans."

Ezekiel rolled his eyes. He had more experience with his mother's bullshit than anyone.

"What do you mean "change of plans"? We made an arrangement," Ferst said.

"I know. But my father—I'm sorry, my stepfather is passing through the city and he will only have tonight to see Zeke."

Ezekiel looked confused. "Granddad is here?"

"Yeah. He is." She answered him with an attitude. Zeke stretched his bottom lip and looked away. He knew what that tone meant. It meant he better shut up and go along with whatever she said.

"Alright." Ferst conceded. "Next time, please let me know in advance. I'm only in town for a couple of days, and I'd like to spend time with my son."

"If you lived here you could spend more time with him. But okay, it's important now that you have three or four days to spare for other people's business?" She was insinuating that the only reason Ferst was visiting was because Joye had business there.

"Alright. I'm not about to do this with you." Ferst turned toward his son, "Zeke? Man, I'll see you tomorrow, okay?" Ferst gave Ezekiel a hug and kissed him on top of his head.

"That's cool Dad. See y'all tomorrow!"

Aubrii had something to prove, Joye was trying to figure out if and how she would deal with this mess her father and Ferst created, and Ferst doesn't drink, but he needed one. Mrs. Allyn was sitting on the sidelines judging all of them. She wanted to be supportive of her daughter, but she had a lot of side-eye and opinions.

Over the next few days, Joye watched Ferst be a dad. It was important yet painful for her. She and her mom spent time enjoying the Bay area. Joye never sat down with Aubrii. She wasn't ready and didn't think it was the best time for them to create a rapport. Joye's first point of business was to find out if Aubrii was really her father's daughter. That would have an impact on how she moved forward. Was she going to end up being a stepmother to her sister's child? Yeah, that could be weird.

She also reminded Ferst that while she had zero concerns about whether she loved him, she wanted to heal her open wounds and resolve matters of the past before officially merging their lives together. She still didn't want to live with him, and she didn't even want to get engaged. Not yet, anyway.

༄

"The lab called. They won't have the results ready before our flights tonight." Joye shared the information with Ferst, her mother, and Ezekiel over dinner.

"So are you and my mom really sisters?" Zeke inquired.

"We may be, Zeke. We don't know yet. What do you think?"

"I dunno. Y'all kinda look alike. A little bit. Dad got a type."

"Ohhh! Really? A type."

"Yeah, man. I got one too. It's all good." Zeke was a cool kid. He had a great personality and was always fun to be around.

"So, Joye? You gonna break up with my dad if y'all are sisters?" Everyone at the table gasped.

Joye was surprised that Ezekiel was bold enough to ask the question, but she enjoyed hearing it. "What do you think I should do, Zeke?"

"I think you should stay with him. My dad never brought a woman around me. He told me he never would unless she was the one." Ezekiel took a gulp of his water. "So, you must be the one. You can't leave." Ezekiel was matter-of-fact in his tone.

"Oh, did your father tell you to say that?"

Ferst shook his head, "The most important people in my life been snitching on me this whole trip. Y'all ain't shit."

"Nah, Dad. I'm just telling you. Plus, I'm thinking about going to college down there or somewhere close to down there. I'd be able to stay at your new house during breaks, right?" Zeke was announcing his approval of Joye and some of his college choices.

Joye smiled, "I would like that. I know your dad would be ecstatic to have you with him more. That's all he talks about; being able to spend time with you."

"Yeah. And maybe he'll put me in one of his movies."

"I want to be in a movie too, Ferst," Mrs. Allyn said. She actually wanted to be an actress but forfeited her dreams when she got married and had children.

The dinner was a nice close to their short and stressful trip before their long flights back to Atlanta and Chicago. Everyone shared a lot of laughs and by the end of the night, they all resorted to making requests for Ferst to put them in movies, buy them things, or asking him if knew famous people.

Joye laughed because she was the ringleader.

"It be your own people," Ferst laughed.

Joye accomplished a few things during her time in the Bay area but not the one thing that initiated the entire trip.

Joye and Aubrii still had to wait just a few more days before the DNA test results would be in. Melanie had completely removed herself from the process. She said no matter what the results were she would never accept Aubrii as her sister. Mrs. Allyn wanted the truth first, and her daughters to be okay with whatever that truth was second. It was business as usual back in Atlanta.

જી

Joye was cooking dinner and told Ferst to come over at about 8:30 p.m. When he arrived she was sitting on her couch with her laptop open.

She didn't budge when he opened the door. She just stared at her screen.

Ferst walked over and gave her a kiss. "Hey, Baby."

She didn't acknowledge his greeting. "Results are in."

"Yeah? What does it say?" Ferst said anxiously.

"I don't know I haven't opened it yet." An air of melancholy surrounded Joye as she managed the anticipation.

Joye moved the laptop and scooted closer to Ferst. She grabbed both of his hands, looked him directly in his eyes, and began to speak. "I don't know what's going to happen. But whatever does happen, and I mean, whatever. I want you to know that I want us to be okay."

"Me too."

"Good. I want to be happy. Even if it isn't perfect and it looks crazy." Joye asked for reassurance, "We can still be happy right?"

"Yes. One hundred percent," Ferst confirmed.

"Good."

Ferst was happy to hear her say that and made it known. "Hmph. I don't think I ever heard you say anything like that before."

"Oh, stop."

"No, it's true. This is the first time since I have known you that you spoke of happiness as more important than perfection. I like it." Ferst leaned in and hugged Joye tight before kissing her on her forehead.

"Well, I've been forfeiting my happiness because of other people's decisions. I'm over it." Joye grabbed her laptop then looked over and pressed the mole on Ferst's right cheek with her index finger. "I've also accepted that humans are nowhere near perfect." She typed in her password.

"Now, let's find out if I have an older sister."

ill[US]ion

Finding [US] in the Illusion

I have experienced so many traumatic events that have shaped me into the woman that I am becoming. I capture them all through the process of journaling as my fight. When I go back and read, I see myself spiraling at many different points and stages of my life and in my relationships. Most people when they talk about me they say, "I'm determined" and I think that's indicative of my fight. But I believe that the fight was a consequence of my mindset that was a consequence of the environment I was placed in resulting in my belief system. An inherited belief system that told me I had to fight for everything I deserved with force and pressure.

Forest has been here for what feels like forever. Our time shared earlier in our lives was amazing. Despite the issues we faced in our first go 'round, we maintained a solid friendship, a profound love for one another, and deep spiritual connection that even when we were broken, it was not.

I'm not surprised that we have picked up where we left off. He was always the guy in waiting meaning it didn't matter who I was with; he forever held space in my heart and in my life. I remember telling him at one point, I don't remember if he was sick, or something was going on and the conversation ended around having no one to take care of him when was old. We were probably joking, but it became an actual thought for me, and I told this man that I would take care of him when was old. That my husband, whoever that might be at that point in my life, would just have to understand. I mean, I entertain the entire process of what that would look like. But it was based on the fact that my love for him was unlike any other. Maybe too real because I don't know one man that would allow that to happen!

Feret knew me on a level that I never allowed anyone to know. I was just comfortable all the time. I don't mean I never got nervous around him or had some physical insecurity, I mean at my core, I was me. I didn't have to pretend.

He helped me work through many difficulties over the years. He has served as a sounding board for almost every hardship I've ever faced and a champion of all of my successes. Because of his own triumphs, he is wisdom, he is sanity, he comedy, he is raw.

In my entry for gaining [CON]trol I talked about why I shouldn't have to fight for what I deserved and now, after finding US in the illusion, I believe that even more now. Now I don't fight as often for the things I deserve, and the reason is because the circumstances, the situations, the environment that I deliberately placed myself in, that Feret has wrapped me in, that I allow others to invite me into, no longer lend themselves to making me have to fight.

The reality is my internal work is shifting my external wellness and most things around me are beginning to offer exactly what I deserve at all times— even the responses that hurt me or make me feel bad. The fight that keeps showing up to beat my ass is a fight I need to heal within. If I can't defeat it there, I can't defeat it anywhere.

about the author

joy alantis

Joy Alantis was born in Chicago, Illinois to the late MacArthur and the great Betty Marshall. She is the mother of Azareah, a Virgo, a middle child, brilliant and funny. Growing up, Joy was in awe of her mother's massive book collection and spent lots of time sneaking off to read them one by one. She read the age-inappropriate books twice!

Joy has survived domestic violence, sexual abuse, and a religious cult. She considers herself a recovering workaholic, a little obsessive-compulsive, and a lot of the definition of #blackgirlmagic. She enjoys spending time with her daughter and grandcat, Apollo Moon, traveling, listening and dancing to music, and watching *almost* good movies for a hearty laugh. She is an adviser to many and takes pride in serving the community through her charitable work with several organizations.

Joy owns shiiift Administrative Management and Consulting and currently lives in Atlanta, Georgia. *The Goddess Journal: dys[FUN]ction* is her first novel.

Contact **Joy Alantis**

WEBSITE	www.dysfunctionbook.com
BLOG	www.joyalantis.com
INSTAGRAM	https://www.instagram.com/joyalantis/
FACEBOOK	https://www.facebook.com/joy.alantis/
TWITTER	https://twitter.com/joyalantis